Johnny Be Good

Keshia C. Willi

House of Honor Books

House of Honor

ISBN: 978-1-68596-047-6

Printed in the United States of America

Published by House of Honor Books.

Harvest, Alabama

DEDICATION

To my shadow.
You are forever the sliver of gray to my little patch of sun.

1 #4...ALMOST

"Take her for a spin," she said. "She drives like the devil and purrs like a kitten."

I didn't really want the car. I was in the market for something else entirely. Don't get me wrong, it was nice, but not as nice as the saleswoman's strawberry blonde curls and legs for miles. I didn't want the car. I wanted her. All the same, I went away emptyhanded that day. It wasn't enough to see her, to take her in like a cool draft, but I wasn't ready. And she wasn't the one.

What do most people see when they look at a woman like her? How pretty she is? The color of her hair? Her sense of style? Probably. I see something different, something taunting my eyes to linger long and hard.

Then, comes the itch.

That grinding, wrenching urge to see what lay inside—the blood, the flesh, the bone of her. Sink my fingers in the red and simply savor it. Most people see the outside, but not many people take the time and pay attention to see what's underneath. I had, and I wanted more.

How's your sight? What do you see when you look at me? Tall and lanky. Long tousled red hair, hanging down to my shoulders, like a limp pile of fallen dead leaves. Dark eyes. Shark eyes, dead inside but always watching. Yeah, that's me. You couldn't pick me out of a lineup or recognize me passing you on the street. I am invisible to the naked eye. A non-entity, I'm a blip in the cosmic forces.

I don't appear to be anything special. It's better that way. You don't know me, and I don't know you. That's why I can tell you the truth. The truth about me. The no holds barred, plain and simple truth. Yeah, maybe I can tell you.

I am, me. I am working my nine to five and going to the bar after work for a cold one. I am sitting on my front lawn just shooting the breeze with nothing to do. There's nothing to see here. I am me, but what you see isn't real.

I am Jekyll and Hyde. Honestly though, I'm much worse. You see, he needed a magic potion to transform into his evil sidekick. I just flip a switch inside and presto! Just like magic—real magic—I am *him*. The man you fear on a dark night in a dark place or a place you shouldn't be.

I am me—slicing and dicing my way through a flirty cocktail waitress like a freaking machine. Turn me off. Turn me on. I keep coming, until there's nothing left of her but a bloody mass of mess. It's *beautiful*.

I am me—crafting my very own jigsaw puzzle out of the voluptuous pieces of a drive-thru goddess. Takeaway and take out, it's bloody delicious.

I am me—sampling the divine red wine of a connoisseur from the local vineyard. Fine dining at its best as I tear into her, bit by glorious bit it's freaking fantastic.

I am me—the One. They are all a part of me. Every one of them now part of the One. I taste their blood every time I remember.

Not nice, you say? Terrible? Fiendish and evil? Perhaps. My mother always said, "Johnny, be good. Make me proud." When she'd say that, I would always smile and nod my head. I was good. I was so very, very good—until I wasn't.

I always thought that being good meant doing everything right. But let's face it, right and wrong are all relative these days. They are different ideas in everybody's minds. So, what's right for you, may be very wrong for me. And what's wrong for you—deeply, egregiously wrong—may be, oh, so very right for me.

The world is one big ant farm, and you have to claw your way to the surface to earn the light, the air and the freedom. When some of those slower ants get in the way, they become a waste of space and oxygen. I eliminate the excess baggage and make room for bigger, better ants, like me.

Women are the easiest prey. Most of them act like gourmet charcuterie when they're just snack-size lunchables in high class disguise. Pathetic, but, oh, so easy to stroke their ego, and whet their appetite for my particular designs. Normally, it wasn't hard to find willing victims. As I said, easy prey. But it had been days, weeks, months since I had found the next "one". The one that was worthy of my special attention. I was hungry. Oh, so very hungry.

I was on the hunt, seeking out the elusive little dove that would satisfy the itch and my starving urges.

Will I find her tonight?

You better, my inner Hyde growled.

Starving for my scarlet fix, the feel of steel against flesh, and the warmth of lifeblood between my fingers, I set out as the sun set. My beat-up old Ford truck was my usual transportation of choice, but that night, I decided to walk. My steady footfalls on the cracked pavement made my heart race. Every step meant I was a breath closer to *Her*. That elusive Her, the dream girl—the one that would light my fire, fuel my needs, and satisfy them. A tall order just for one girl, I know. I was young. I was ambitious and I was *hungry*. I needed to flip the switch and let Hyde out to play. He was hungry too.

The walk was peaceful and quiet. In that sleepy town, not much happened after seven at night. Only the young would venture out for their amusements.

Sneaking into R-rated movies at the little drive-in theater. Parking at the abandoned meat factory. Or perhaps, just milling around the side streets and alleys. The posh, the popular and the less than desirable mingled as one. The odds of pairing off within such an odd mix weren't great. Still, it was enough for the wonderfully weird to find a few moments of dreamed of bliss.

There was a particular spot that was an adolescent party speedway. Anyone and everyone knew about it, even the adults, though no one would admit it. It was the town's little secret from itself. A place of drugs, temporary love, and any other fix you might need in the cover of night.

I was headed there. I had tried my hand there before with little success. I once got a girl to follow me home. She went as far as my front step, before she got wise, made her excuses and left.

So close and yet so damn far.

That night I drank myself to sleep and wallowed in the festering urge that had not been satisfied. I dreamed that night of delicate flesh and the color red, but my eager hands were empty. I promised myself that this time would be different. So, this time I wouldn't go emptyhanded. I wouldn't rush the lure. I'd let the trap play out. Every move was integral. Every word, every step, every smile, and touch were vital. I'd reach the final end of flesh, blood, and bone. I'd drink all of it in, gorging myself on a piece of sweetness and power.

Steady now, Johnny. Don't get too excited. Not yet.

I took a deep breath that tumbled from my mouth like a weight ready to sink to the bottom of the sea. I was deep into myself now.

Don't go too far.

I broke away from my thoughts, climbing out of the mire and the gutter of my desire. Deep breath in. Deep breath out.

Much better.

My body was on fire, but my head was cool. Cool, calm, and collected again, I was ready. Damn, was I ready. My body began to move with a confident swagger. I strutted down the street toward the abandoned mall parking lot like a god. I am me, King of the night. At least, I would be once I had Her. For the moment, I was hanging on to the Hyde switch. Hanging onto it like a drunken idiot waiting to flip it. Then the light would go on in my dead, dark eyes. I'd feel myself come alive inside and out.

My body had now upgraded from a steady burn to the itch that seemed ready to rip my insides to shreds if I waited much longer. I was used to the burn and the urge. The itch was something more, worse. Sometimes, for all my efforts, the itch could not be scratched or contained. I am addicted to the very deep, visceral pleasure and pain that erupts when I meet with the success of a trap well-laid, and the lure taken.

I reached the spot, breathless and anxious, my body alert and trembling. It was already littered with people. Girls, girls, girls. Everywhere.

Now, now, Johnny. Be good.

The words coaxed me back to myself.

Slow it down, Johnny, and you'll be good.

I was, ready to plunge headfirst into this mass of bodies, but that wasn't how this should be done. It was a delicate operation, a complicated dance between predator and prey. A titillating intercourse between body and body, until both could understand the other's rhythm. Sense the eagerness and the wanting. Then—then it was time to strike.

Easy, boy. You're getting ahead of yourself just now.

I slowed my steps to a slithering crawl as I approached the crowd. They were just miserable little ants trying to scramble up to the light. They thought they knew the dark, but they didn't know dark like mine. I could muster up a façade that resembled the light they sought.

Oh, how they crave the light.

I could be good. I could be *real* good. I stopped to take in the many bodies that had collected so deliciously at my feet. It was almost like they knew. Like they could hear the longing and the need in me, and they came. There were so, so many of them. It was glorious.

I didn't look at faces. Faces mean nothing. If anything, they were a distraction from the real show. Those rose-tinted cheeks and sugar-plum lips were just their own sort of pathetic lure. The only one to which most of them paid attention. Meanwhile, the rest of themselves they let go to hell. Their pale, chicken legs, were speckled with dark hairs and bared for the world to see in short, short skirts. Their skinny, bony arms looked more like a skeleton with skin then real *flesh*. The teased and over-gelled hair, were it free of its wretched condiments, would be a delightful treat on the right girl. Hips that were overwhelmed by a sea of breastless torsos, these girls were trash meant to be discarded.

Then, there were the jewels, the lovelies that rise above the rest of the muck. They were incomparable beauties, their bodies like temples, pure and unadulterated. Silky smooth and perfectly perfect in every way that it was not enough just to look at this sort. No, I had to taste them. I had to devour that tender beauty until I had gnawed them down to gristle. Their superficial goddess complex consumed leaving a bone-dry arid mess of pretty leftovers that were only a shadow of what once was.

That sort of diamond among the rust and the dust was hard to find. I searched the mess of people for such a one, hoping I would finally get lucky. This had to be the night.

It had better be, Hyde reminded me.

I began to make my way through the cluttered crowd, my eyes open wide, my mind alert. My heart nearly beat out of my chest.

Keep it cool, Johnny Boy. Keep it cool.

Deep breath in. Deep breath out.

My mind recharged in an instant and I was ready. I powered through the crowd like a monster truck, revving up my engine for the big finish. Many of the girls clung to a boy as if they were going out of style. An over-eager son of a bitch would go after those. They're easy prey, and just plain easy. They want whatever you've got and whatever you're willing to give them.

They were hungry too, starving in their own way. It didn't mean it was special, just meant it was free. Free attention and free feels, all so she can brave to look at herself with confidence in the morning. No, these were far too easy sheep to skin. I wanted a challenge, and so, I went after the girls that stuck together. Alone, they were the brave and independent bitches who had, in their words, no need for men who couldn't give them what they wanted or thought they deserved.

These were the crème de la crème of prizes for a guy like me, because to bag one of these, you had to think smart. You couldn't just come on strong and overwhelm them with compliments and sickeningly sweet sentiment. These girls were real. They were tough. Tough to crack and tough to lure, but I was up for the challenge.

I zeroed in on a small gaggle of these girls near a dingy, rusted out trash bin fire. They passed around a shiny new metal flask and spoke in low tones. They looked serious, gossiping among themselves. Women's troubles, and old boyfriends held up on a pike, skinned alive and exposed for everyone in their vicious circle to see and judge. That image burned into my mind, and I took a step back.

Can I really take one of these down?

I licked my lips, imagining how I'd do it. As I haplessly daydreamed of my sweet nightmare, I caught the attention of one of these girls. She eyed me strangely, with a look of disdain, perhaps it was even disgust. That tripped me up. She was independent *and* smart.

Damn.

I imagined from her look that she could see right through me to my bloody-red intentions. She continued to stare, unabashed and unafraid.

Damn, have I met my match?

I shrunk when I stood beneath her glare. Almost lost my nerve, and then—

"Hey, what are you staring at?" she demanded.

Her voice was low, much lower than I had guessed. It had a sexy rasp to it that made it seem like she was permanently pissed. Maybe she was. Tongue-tied, I lost my cool. I didn't answer.

She handed the flask to one of the other girls and began to walk toward me. No, strut is the right word. Despite her efforts to look less than impressive in her baggy shirt dress, the way her hidden body shifted— oh, so subtly—beneath the cool cotton fabric was instantly seductive. Yes, she was lovely. Not like the rest, whose wide eagle eyes gawked at me from their stony perch.

Her eyes were on me, and I met them with a confidence that could only have seeped in from the deep realm of desire. The itch was bubbling to the surface, preparing for the full effect. If I could just get my hands on her, the real dark would come.

"Did you hear me?" she asked loudly.

She was standing right in front of me now. She was shorter than me by more than a foot, but she wore her small stature like a weapon. She was ready to do battle. Unlike the other girls in this godforsaken gutter, she wasn't here for a quick fix or a statement to the world. I could see that. Oh no, she was here against her will, probably dragged here by one of those other little chits standing behind her.

This unique girl was chewing hard on a piece of gum. She rolled it under her tongue to talk to me. I watched her bubble gum tongue lick her bare lips, naturally stained a subtle mauve.

"You talk, or what?" she asked.

Hyde was toying with the switch inside me now, so dangerously close to pumping it up and on.

Catch her first, big boy. Time's a-wasting.

I plastered a big plastic smile across my face, cocking my head to the side with a glint of mischief in my dark shark eyes that were always hunting, always hungry.

"Of course," I said in a velvety smooth voice. "What would you like me to say?"

The girl with the bubble gum tongue looked me up and down, and smiled as she cocked her head to the side to meet my eyes.

"Hmm," she murmured, rolling her gum around in her mouth with a playful flick of her tongue that was just for me. She smiled. That was for me too. "Let me think."

I sighed inwardly. Hyde was getting anxious, and she was going to play this out for all it was worth.

Slow and steady, Johnny. But get her moving!

I gave her a sultry half-smile and waited, oh so patiently, as she made up her freaking mind what she would say next. I watched her intently and saw as the lightbulb flicked on in her diminutive, little hairspray-congested mind. God, this was going to be slow. Her goddess like looks, it seemed, had over-exaggerated her mental capacity. I gauged by her silence that she was as flimsy and fragile in the mind as her ridiculous friends.

"Tell me I'm pretty," she finally said softly, edging closer to me.

The scent of her cheap perfume wafted to my

nostrils. It was pungent but still seductive to an eager me. She must really be desperate fishing for free compliments already. Perhaps I had overestimated her. Maybe she wasn't a chosen goddess, but one of those cheap thrills and frills girls, ready for anything if it meant nothing. She wasn't Her, not my goddess. But the itch was already in high gear. Hyde was ready to take over. She would have to do. I stepped too close to her, my chest nearly brushing her bosom.

"You're pretty," I answered just as softly.

She smiled, just what she wanted to hear.

Good, boy. Good.

"You really think so?" She delicately played with her tangle of black teased hair. She pushed her body against mine. Her eyes glinted wild in the light of the trash bin fire. "What else?"

God, this is easy.

"I could tell you more, but..."

I let my words trail off for dramatic effect. She took the bait. Her glitter-bombed eyes suddenly looked sad, as her naked lips bounced into a playful pout.

"But what?" She took in the lure.

She rolled on her heels until her body rocked back and forth, ebbing and flowing. Her chest pressed so softly into mine.

Damn, this is too easy.

Go ahead, boy, Hyde demanded.

I pressed my body close to hers. The bubble gum tongue licked her lips hard, as her mouth slowly parted, just a little, just enough. Her eyes were wide and hungry. Now for the real bait.

"But I'd rather show you," I whispered.

She leaned in dangerously close to hear it, before glancing back at her glowering gaggle of friends. They were jealous. I could tell. She could tell, and she liked it. Her head whipped back to me, her long hair flipping as she did. A smile slowly curled around the corners of her lips.

"Alright, then," she said soft and low.

Bait taken.

Before I had time to say anything in return, she held out her delicate hand to me. I looked at her. Looked at her offered hand. Here was everything I wanted being laid out on a silver freaking platter for me. It was beautiful. She was beautiful. Goddess or no goddess.

Don't you want it, Johnny? Don't you want her?

"Yes," The word tumbled out of my mouth in answer before I could catch it.

I blushed in embarrassment, but quickly covered it up with a look of sheer and utter desire, which I could tell left her wanting more. It wasn't really desire; it was hunger. The urge had broken out into the itch and the itch had painfully burst into something bigger. Something harder to contain.

I grabbed her hand and pulled her away from her gawking, four-eyed friends, who I could guarantee weren't getting anything tonight. We moved away from the trash bin fires and the obnoxiously loud crowd, out into the clear night. The air was still and heavy with humidity and the heat from the day.

She followed willingly at first, her hand loose in mine, molding to my own tight grip. It was too tight, I knew, but she didn't seem to mind. We marched through the back alleyways and the lonely streets, further and further away from the crowd, the noise, and her friends. I began to feel her pulling away from my touch. She was hesitant and strangely silent.

Ease up, Johnny. Ease up, or you'll lose her.

I didn't listen to my own advice this time. I never listened when I was this close to getting what I wanted. What I needed and what Hyde had to have.

"Where are we going?" she said quietly.

She sounded afraid, and so I turned back to look at her. Her lips were clamped shut into a sour frown, her bubble gum tongue had all but disappeared and her eyes were wide and unabashedly wary. She was afraid.

Damn, this isn't working.

I tried smiling at her, easing my grip on her hand. I tried to make her more comfortable next to my own burning skin.

"We're almost there," I said softly, but still there was an urgency in my voice I could not contain.

She wasn't having it. I knew she could hear the strangeness in my voice, see the eerie wildness glinting in my dead eyes. She wasn't stupid after all, just a little slow to catch on. Slowly, she started to pull away, but my grip on her was ironclad. I wasn't going to let her get away, not this one, not this time. Goddess or no, she was going to be mine. I couldn't wait for Her, for that unreachable perfection that eluded me. My body, my mind, had to be satisfied by something.

We had reached my street with her struggling even more. I didn't want a freaking scene. She was hell-bent on making one. We were yards away from my house, its faint and flickering porch light surrounded by moths. It flashed like a warning sign that caught my eye. I knew then that this wasn't going to end well.

I pulled her up the sidewalk, regretting my choice. She wasn't what I wanted. She wasn't what I needed. I marched closer and closer to my glorious haven, with my bounty in reluctant tow.

Suddenly, I stumbled. My grip on the girl was lost as I tumbled to the pavement. As I hit the ground hard, I felt her fingers slip away, pull away hastily, as if the touch of my burning skin was something grotesque and disgusting. She was gone. Scurrying away from the flickering buggy light cast from my front porch and out into the gathering shadow of the night. I could hear her hollow clip-clapping footsteps even after she had long disappeared. Soon, even that was gone, and I was left alone.

I sighed, realizing I was still lying dumbfounded on

the sidewalk. I scrambled to my feet, not caring to brush myself off or glance down at my scraped knee. As I hobbled to my front door, I could feel the warm blood oozing down my leg. Slow like honey, but not as sweet, not mine. I wasn't so desperate as to find my own blood intoxicating, it was only a nuisance and a mess.

Hyde had gone silent when he realized he wasn't getting a show or any satisfaction. He had hidden away in the forgotten folds of my hapless mind, that were bumbling to remember how to open the door.

Key first, dumbass.

Key first, right. The door slid open as the key slipped inside the lock and turned. I stood in the doorway, staring into the shadows and the nothingness. I was alone in the night.

2 Downtime and Downplaying...

Days. Weeks. Months.
Morning.

It's my favorite time of day. There's time to think, time to dream and time to plan. Lately, my brain was all dried up and switched off—numb from too much time alone, unoccupied and starving. I was a ghost of myself, a soggy remnant of a better man, all chewed up and with nowhere to go. I had lost my touch just as I had found it. There had barely been time to relish it, to savor its sweetness before fate stepped in and crushed it. Now I had nothing but white-knuckled fists, posed to fight, but, meh—not really in the mood. These days, I wasn't in the mood for anything. I pushed myself to go to work every day.

Gotta keep up appearances.

I made myself eat, along with the steady supply of beer.

Gotta stay alive.

But why? I had lost my sense of Her, lost her completely. I'd lost the desire and the craving for Her. She wasn't real—couldn't be.

Never say never.

"Quiet," I mumbled to the no one in my brain as I crawled onto my belly in the bed, clutching to my lone pillow like it was my lover.

My eyes blinked in the sharp morning light shearing through the broken plastic blinds. Dazed, I stared it down, despite the blinding, searing pain. I wanted the pain. I wanted it to turn into some kind of pleasure or awakening. Anything, so long as *I felt* something. I had been too long in the land of numb. I waited, expecting transformation, and getting none. All I had was a headache and a deep shadow line burned into my vision. I slumped my head over the side of the bare mattress, following the pattern of light-infused dust that sailed and fluttered in the air before me. I watched each particle fall and gently settle on the ratty shag carpet and I sighed.

Had I really come to this? Was I really a failure before I had even gotten started? Was I going to starve and die in this room? There was no internal answer. The voices in my head had gone quiet.

Figures.

When I actually needed help, they were out of ideas. When the chips were down and desperation was lying on the table, myself ready to be slaughtered, they had nothing to say. Damn, stupid—

Oh, hello. What's this?

A quiet sound in the recesses of my mind began to flutter to the surface. Gently it peeled back the folds of my brain, clawing at the delicate and raw membrane, and getting louder and louder as it climbed to the top. It sat there, slowly coming into focus, slowly rising to my naked ears. And then—Hyde!

No wonder you haven't bagged your prize. Look at you. Look at this place. Disgusting. Pathetic. Unimaginative. A laugh. You couldn't catch a fly if your tongue was made of sugar.

I was quiet now. Whatever had invaded my mind was right. I was still fumbling in the dark when it came to my passion project. It had been all consuming and I had been impatient, unwilling to master my craft but rather make a mockery of the rage and the artistry it inspired. I had wanted to be a master, a true artist of flesh and blood and bone. Instead, I was a laughingstock.

There I was, lying nearly naked in the tepid morning sun, feeling sorry for myself when there was so much to be done. My place was a mess of takeout boxes and beer cans and dirty magazines. It wasn't fit for company, and certainly not for the likes of Her. A girl the likes of Her would be disgusted, appalled even—

And we can't have that.

No, Mr. Hyde, we couldn't have that. So, I scrambled out of my lair, pulled on whatever boxers I could find, and dragged myself to the bathroom.

My, my, Johnny. You've really let yourself go. But we can fix that.

I eyed my pale unshaven face, my long-mussed hair, and my red-veined eyes in the cracked bathroom mirror. I grimaced. I was a mess. A sloppy and unpolished stone lost in an ocean on its own. I began to realize just what this endless search for perfection had done to me. The perfect woman, the perfect offering to my desire and my need had made me come completely undone.

Damn her.

"What?" I whispered, forgetting that I was merely answering myself. But the suddenness of the change, the subtle anger that swept over me at the echo of those words within the quiet of my mind curled my lips into a devilish grin. I looked like a ghoulish specter, as I stared myself down, the anger growing.

Yes, it was that Her, that infamous Her, unattainable and hidden from me that had ruined me. It was Her fault.

Damn her.

"Damn her," I repeated soft and low.

My breathing was already quickening, my heartbeat racing as my mind stuttered to life again.

I was *back*.

The shame and embarrassment of my last foolish attempt was pushed away and forgotten. I was me again, but I had to be better—better than the old me. Better at controlling myself, better at stalking, better at catching, and better at killing.

I had to be much better at hiding in plain sight. A part of everything but separated just enough to keep me from going soft. I needed to harness whatever hatred I had for the last girl, for every girl I'd ever touched or laid my eyes on and turn it into power. Fuel for the fire inside me, until it raged and roared and consumed me. Yeah, my pathetic flickering flame was hungry. It needed fuel.

So, I set about doing research. You know the kind. The watching kind, the kind that stupid kids always get caught doing. Why? Because they're kids and they're not that smart when it comes to things like smut-snooping, as I liked to call it. Of course, I don't think it's wrong to peer into lighted windows and open blinds. The dark of the night covers me, cloaks me all in black until I am a part of it. The night and the darkness.

No one thinks to look at their window in the night. But everyone knows—knows that it's a free show for the taking. Those girls know what they're doing when they carelessly leave those window shades up, the flimsy curtains parted just a crack. They do it anyway. Why? Because they like the thrill, the dangerous niggle in the back of their minds that says, "Someone could be watching me." They want you to watch.

I'm happy to oblige them, provided they're worth looking at. When it comes to peep shows, even the grotesquely large seem to think that a bit of lace in all the wrong places will erase an amorphous error in human creation. The things hiding behind those windows are enough to turn my stomach. They leave me starving for the real thing, that goddess shape that haunts my nightmares and my daydreams. It is all-consuming. Like fire in a trash bin, it burns what's inside and scars what's outside until all you can see is what the fire has touched. Needless to say, I was particular about which windows I chose for my evening's delights and escapades, and very, very careful. I usually stuck to my neighborhood.

***

Tonight—tonight I felt the wolf-like need to wander aimlessly to see just what I could find out there in the darkness. The moon slipped seductively into her low hanging perch, heavy-laden and burgeoning with naked energy. I could feel the desire and the hunger hanging in the air. Or maybe it all came from me. I couldn't tell.

Easy, boy. Remember, look, but don't touch.

That was easier said than done. My fingers were itching to wrap themselves in female flesh.

Red. All red.

"Whoa, easy," I told myself, and it startled me.

I was inches away from too close. I slowed my pace as I walked, nearly tripped on my way down the hot, crackling sidewalk. The day was one of the hottest of the summer, but the night was becoming a chilly relief from the wall of intense heat that still hovered about me. Slowing my steps brought a cool breath of pavement-scented breeze. I breathed it in, letting it ease my alert and anxious mind. I tried to take in the world around me. I wasn't the only one crawling out from under my hot rock.

Bleary-eyed youngsters stumbled out of open garages and back screen doors, bringing with them the strong scents of summer funk. Young lovers crept quietly out, strolling hand in hand, doe-eyed and stupid. And then, there were the young women, herding through the street in loud, yappy flocks with little or no direction. A constant stream of beautiful nothings, aimless lovelies that caught my eye like streamers in a parade. Yes, it was certainly a parade of pretty little things. I could take my pick, take any one I wanted.

Right here. Right now. Hyde reached for the switch.

Ah, but that's against the rules, boy. Remember. Look, but don't touch.

Look at the fresh and supple bodies, the delicate curves and bouncing breasts. Look at those long, luscious legs, and don't forget that ass.

Look, but don't touch.

I could feel my hunger rising up like acid in my throat. I choked it back and veered my eyes away. I dodged the beauties on their wandering treks and headed down an alleyway. Breathless, I stopped, leaning headfirst on the brick wall of the building.

Breathing was about all I could do.

Breathe. Just breathe.

Turns out that night the temptation was too much—too impossible to ignore. It rushed up to meet me in a wave, a sweet and intoxicating, but deadly wave. Oh, so deadly. It would be the death of me if I gave in. The me that was fettered to this hunger would break if it was not fed.

"Please," I begged weakly, hungrily.

Silence answered.

"Please," I pleaded again, beating the brick wall with my bare fist until my knuckles bled. "Let me play."

You wanna play?

"Yes."

You wanna play?

"Yes!" My voice echoed in the empty alleyway.

Silence. And then—

Wait.

I sighed, close to tears. The breath tumbling clumsily off my lips trembled like a weighted blanket drawn from my lungs.

Wait.

My dirty fingernails dug at the brick until it crumbled. I couldn't breathe, couldn't think.

I screamed. I don't remember anymore.

3 A NEW SLATE

*Y*ou're not having much luck now, are you?
I stared myself down in the cracked bathroom mirror, my naked body glistening with sweat. My chest heaving with heavy breaths.

"No," I muttered reluctantly.

Maybe this isn't for you. Hyde suggested.

"It is," I argued back.

No.

"But—"

No. You're weak, clumsy. You're too caught up in your feelings to listen to your brain. Your instinct. Damn you.

"No."

Damn you.

I gritted my teeth, trembling in anger. "Damn you," I muttered quietly.

What's that? I didn't hear you.

"I said—" I started softly.

Speak louder, boy. Speak. Speak!

"Damn you!" I screamed.

The room went silent.

It was so quiet I could hear my heart pulsing in my ears. I wasn't ready for the quiet. A silence so deep that even my own thoughts seemed to retract into the folds of my sinewy consciousness, leaving me alone. In a flash of rage, I recalled them, pushed them back to the forefront. I stared them down and made them speak. If anything, to avoid the silence. I gritted my teeth.

"I said—*damn you.*"

I waited for a reaction, staring myself down defiantly in the mirror.

You think you can do it?

I had. Didn't that count? I had taken life, tasted blood. Like a freaking god, I felt life slip through my fingers as I crushed it.

I didn't need to answer Hyde's sneering voice. It knew my answer.

Prove it then.

Alright, I would. If I could only get out of this damned small town.

Fall came without Her, without anyone. I settled into a monotonous routine. Work. Bar. Home. Sleep. Repeat.

On weekends, the routine was much the same, minus the work, more bar, less sleeping. All of it was done alone. No lovelies. No maybes. *Nada.* Didn't even see anything to tempt my eye. Every woman's face was just another face. An empty canvas that I didn't care to write my name anywhere on.

That's not to say I didn't try. I let my glance wander where it would. But she wasn't there. That's when I realized that I would never find her here. The pickings were too slim. The herd was too small. What lovelies there were had gotten wise and drifted inside as the cold of grip of winter threatened.

Mind you, she might have vanished with the coming cold, but the memory of her was singed into my every fiber, every inch of my flesh. Somewhere underneath those thick cotton ball coats and tall, tall boots was the one.

I needed a change of scenery. I needed somewhere new, warm, and bright. Mr. Hyde, crouching just below the surface, impatiently biding his time, seemed to agree. His dirty hand creeping slowly toward that switch.

Turn me on. Go ahead. Try it. I dared him.

Hungry. So hungry.

So, I packed what little I owned into my old Ford truck and kissed that sorry ass small town goodbye. As I watched it disappear in the rearview mirror, I caught a taste of my own reflection, burning deep red in the bloody light of the setting sun. Caught myself as I cocked a smile on my pale thin lips.

Be good and say goodbye, Johnny. Mother's voice chided.

Goodbye.

New me. New city. And traffic.

The first sight of my new hometown was wall to wall traffic for miles ahead of me and miles behind. A lukewarm blanket of half-dead air conditioning blasted through my car. By the time I reached the city's welcome sign, I was hot and bothered, ready to jump out of that truck into the oncoming four-lanes of traffic. I was itching to move, to walk, to do anything other than sit in that damn truck listening to the Top 40 on a loop.

I hated music—all of it. At least, I hadn't found any that appealed to my dark and constantly reeling mind. Music was meant to soothe the savage beast. Yeah, right. It just made me anxious, peeling away what little feelings I had and pushing back the freedom of thought I had learned to allow myself. It left in its rotted and festering wake a me I didn't want to see.

With a constipated groan, I flipped the radio off. Silence, at least the kind of quiet that comes from loud trucks on loud highways with a million angry people behind the wheel. That's a million and one, if you included me. I was certainly stuck, and I was certainly angry.

Loud blasts of distant car horns came bursting through my open windows. Like a wave, they rushed toward me, up the line and passed me. Not wanting to be left out, I honked my horn in answer. I chuckled to myself at the thought of those sweating, churlish roadworkers getting a rush of that animosity. All of it, every ounce of it, meant for them.

I let my hand hang out of the window, feeling the sticky early summer air clamp onto my damp skin. Just like that, like Moses parting the damn Red Sea with the flick of his wrist, the traffic began to move. I chuckled again at my own magic and put my car back in drive. On my way again, I noticed the car riding beside me was full of girls. Not pretty, but still easy on the eyes. They giggled and laughed as they blasted the Top 40 on its loop, singing along to every song. Just for laughs, I flipped my radio back on, turning the volume up to the brink of exploding my old speakers. I caught their eye, and they caught mine.

Smile, stupid.

So, I did. They smiled back, giggling all the while, but it was just a tease. An appetizer for what was coming for me in this new place. I decided to tease right back. With a laugh, I put the pedal to the metal and sped off toward my new start.

4 HUNGRY...AGAIN

Blood. I was standing in her blood. It was pooling all around me, seeping into my favorite sneakers until my socks gave a viscous squish as I gingerly stepped around her body. #4—not exactly the one and not exactly how I wanted to start things off in my new hometown.

I found her on the first day as I came to the city, bright-eyed and bushy tailed. I was ready for something different, something infinitely better. As I pulled into a gas station, I asked the attendant for directions and bought a pack of cigarettes and a Yoohoo. It was not quite the celebratory fare I had hoped for, but then, there wasn't a decent beer to be found. Besides, I wanted to keep my head clear, and my eyes and ears open to take in every new sight and sound. I wanted this virginal drive through the city to be special.

But then, *She* appeared. She sidled up to the counter just as I laid my items down. Shoving mine aside, she made room for her sanitary pads, cigarettes, and the bag of Twizzlers, from which she was already eating. She gave me a saucy, pissed off look as she gnawed on her candy like a cow on its cud. Her mouth hung open and bits of Twizzler stuck to her teeth. I stared at her, and she stared back at me, loudly drumming her chipped red fingernails on the counter. The stupid cashier didn't know who to favor. So, she made the decision for him.

Turning to the old man, she said bluntly, "Ding,

ding, ding! Ring me up, old man. It's kinda an emergency!" She glanced down at the pads.

The cashier gave me an apologetic frown as he began to ring up the girl's items. I was cool. I wasn't angry. There was something about that girl that rubbed me the wrong way. Maybe it was her mussed and matted brown hair. Her three-day-old makeup that stained and caked her average-looking face. Or perhaps it was her frayed and ripped t-shirt. I never did like Pink Floyd. Or maybe it was a combination of all these things and the simmering heat of the evening. Whatever it was, it agitated me, tugged and plucked at my fibrous nerves until they vibrated with a sort-of steady beat of anger. Hunger, not anger.

The heat must have been getting to me. Because, as this girl grabbed her plastic bag from the old man behind the counter and gave him a little sneer, Mr. Hyde flipped the freaking switch. I didn't want her. But I had to have her.

I turned my attention to her as she walked away, my eyes sharp and awake. I imagined they must have had a hungry gleam to them, because the old man hurried about ringing up my purchase. His palsied hand slid my items across the counter, and with a narrowed glare, he nodded. It was an invitation to play that game of niceties; disingenuous and neatly packaged like humanity. I smiled and gave him a nod as I grabbed my things and walked out.

I was immediately blasted by the heat. It was like hitting a brick wall with my face. My body tensed. Where was the girl? I searched the nearly vacant parking lot. Billows of dust floated across the pavement with a warning hiss. Everything—the smell of the air, the red setting sun, the silence—seemed off. Wrong somehow. I should have been alert. I should have listened to the warning so clearly screaming out from the universe. But I didn't. Instead, I heard—

"You got a car?"

It was the girl from the store. I turned around and saw her leaning against the crumbling, faded brick of the building. Her bag of Twizzlers was nearly finished. The rest of her items were still in the white plastic shopping bag slung across her wrist. She was still chewing, her wide mouth opening and closing with a noisy squish. It was like her jaw was about to dislocate. I noticed now that she had a pair of metal braces stuck to her teeth. No wonder she chewed like a barn animal.

My stomach turned at the sight of her. But somehow my disgust must have looked to her like interest, because she said, "Can I bum a ride?"

Go on, boy. It might be fun.

I had barely nodded when she popped up from her perch against the wall and strutted toward me, hips swinging. She had a certain bounce to her skin-and-bones figure. There wasn't much to her: no chest, no backside, no curvature. A pathetic excuse for femininity without a hint of an hourglass design to her form.

But there she was, riding shotgun in my beat-up truck and staring out of the window in silence as we drove. She had switched from Twizzlers to gum. I preferred the Twizzlers to the lip-smacking and saliva-squishing of her busy mouth with that gum. It ground on my nerves, putting me even more on edge.

To stop the noise, I decided to make small talk. No easy feat in this quiet, but I was up to the challenge. I turned to her. The wind from the open car windows was whipping through her hair. I could smell a hint of body odor wafting from her side of the car. It twinged and burned my nostrils, and it took all I had to keep from gagging. I had never smelled something so ripe and rancid coming off something alive. Instead of the girl being ashamed or embarrassed, she kicked off her ratty sneakers and propped her filthy feet on my dashboard. She laid her head in her hand on the open window as she looked back at me. Her underarm brazenly displayed a heavy blanket of bronze peach fuzz. She knew that it bothered me. Knew I had no interest in the filth she had to offer. So, she flaunted it.

I took a deep breath through my open mouth, avoiding the smell, though I felt like I could taste it on the air.

Look at her, boy. Look at her. Ugly as sin and a mockery of everything we want.

"Where exactly am I taking you, um—"

She hadn't given me her name. She smiled at my fumbling for words, and cackled, a shrill and disgusting sound.

"As long as we're not going back to your place, you can drive me anywhere, honey," she said.

"Don't have a place...yet," I muttered.

"You just get to town?"

I turned my eyes back to the road. I didn't want to look at her anymore. She made my stomach sick.

"Yeah. Just moved here."

She eyed me with the first ounce of sincerity I'd seen on her dumb face and announced, "I don't either."

She gave a heavy exaggerated sigh. Full of meaning I could sense but didn't understand.

"Home's overrated. The open road. That's where it's at."

She dug a cigarette from her jeans' pocket. It was partially smoked and saved. Probably her last. She scooted her butt up in the seat and dug in her back pocket for a lighter.

"Shit!" She muttered.

I pointed toward the glove compartment. "There's a lighter in there."

She popped it open. She had no qualms rifling through my personal things inside. She found my wallet and took a peek, giggling at my driver's license picture. She held it closer to her face to read my name.

"Johnny. Your name is Johnny?" She looked at me with a smile. It felt mocking. I hated her all the more.

I didn't answer. Instead, I tried to grab the wallet from her, but she held it out of my reach. Her eyes narrowed. Watching me closely, she dug into the wallet and pulled out what little money there was left in it. With a dramatic flair and seductive eyes, her thin lips pursed in a sexy smile. Holding it between two fingers, she wedged the cash between her breasts. As if I'd go digging for it there.

Hurry up, boy. Time's a-wasting. Hyde was getting impatient.

"You from around here?" I asked.

She seemed thrown off by the question. And so, I asked something different. "You know anyone from around here?"

The girl seemed uncomfortable now. She shook her head slowly. I spotted a forested area up ahead with a rest stop. It was empty. Probably no longer used at all.

Perfect.

"Good," I said and swerved the truck off the road to the rest stop. The truck came to a screeching stop. The girl nearly rammed headfirst into the windshield. I was a bit disappointed that she hadn't. It would have saved me the trouble of finishing her off myself.

Isn't that your job?

Yes, I thought.

I can't hear you. Isn't that your job, boy?

Aloud, I muttered, "Yes."

My eyes were on the girl, intensely and with intent. Our eyes met, and I swear to God, she knew. Could sense the hunger dripping off me. Me? I could smell the scent of fear on her rancid body. I leaned toward her. She gasped and leaned up against the door. Her arms flailed back, hitting the open air.

"Relax," I said softly, reaching between her legs to the seat underneath.

Johnny, be good.

"You can go in a minute. But first, I want to show you something." I smiled, my arm lingering between her bony legs.

She peered nervously down, gulping hard. At that moment, she could have passed for pretty. Her lips wobbled, and she stuttered, "W-w-what?"

I kept my plastic smile plastered on my sweaty face. Slowly I brought up my hand.

Slowly. Slowly. Relish every damn second.

Slowly, I brought up my hand. The hand that held the knife. The knife I always kept at the ready for just such an occasion. I watched her eyes go big as saucers. I brought it up to her skin. Her chest. Her neck. I let it linger there. Slowly sliding it across her throbbing skin. I could feel her pulse beating wildly through the metal of the blade. It was that hard and fast. My senses were keen, sharp, alive. I could feel her every breath, every heartbeat, hear every thought running through that derelict little brain of hers. I breathed her in to feel her now.

I felt myself retreating into my own mind, a dark and sterile waiting room of sinewy silence. There I could observe everything without getting caught up in feelings or conscience. After all, this was my silent place. There was no room for thought or emotion.

That was Hyde's cue to go to work. He had waited so long, so patiently. Now, he was hungry. Oh, so very hungry. Starving. Famished. He would not be sated until he'd had her.

I leaned in close to her grotesquely fragrant body and whispered, "Run."

But she didn't. She didn't do anything but blubber and cry. What a disappointment! She teased me, taunted me with a good chase, only to fizzle out in a cool, damp shower of tears. I knew that this was going to be messy even before I started.

Show her, Johnny.

I took the knife and pantomimed my intentions

with it against my own neck. Quick and fast. See? You won't even feel it—promise. Of course, I was lying through my teeth. It would be quick, but it wouldn't be painless. I didn't want it to be. I wanted the little chit to feel every inch of the scar I was going to give her.

I watched her eyes as she realized that. She quickly fumbled for the door handle. Finding it, she burst through the door and tumbled out onto the gravel, skinning both her knees. Blood ran down to her ankles. She ran, alright. Into the abandoned rest stop. Probably looking in desperation for anyone who might still be there. Foolishly, she glanced back, stumbling forward on the pavement as she did.

They always look back. Every damn time.

"They always do," I muttered to the ether in my brain.

I put a finger to my lips to quiet them, and then I stepped out of my car. I took my time, each step a brand-new step closer to a good time. My body was on edge. Alert and full to the brim with anticipation for what was to come, for the inevitable outcome of this little charade.

The sun was beginning to set painting the skyline a delicious candy apple red. There was not a car to be seen. That surprised me. For a busy metropolitan area, it seemed to roll up the carpet and settle in quite early. Perhaps it was the heat. Sweat was dripping off me in steady rain. I kept the knife close to my body and relatively out of sight. Though the place was empty, except for the girl and me. Still, I didn't want to take any chances.

Gotta play it smart.

I caught sight of her slipping into the ladies' bathroom. The door stood ajar. She hadn't turned the lights on. Probably no power or she was smarter than she looked? But she wasn't smart enough to make herself invisible, not like I could. She was very easy to find and very easy to kill.

I opened the restroom door just a little wider, just wide enough for me to slip through quietly. Thank God, the door didn't screech and howl. Some old doors do if they're left unused. I had learned that the hard way. I tiptoed my way into the restroom. It was all dark shadows and the red of the fading sunlight painting everything that beautiful color. I stopped to take a look around. I scanned the bottom panels of the stalls for feet and found none.

A little game. Hunt her! Hunt her!

Hyde was getting louder and more urgent. I couldn't hold him back much longer. I gripped the knife tighter as I ever so quietly made my way over to each stall, pushing open door after door, after door. Nothing. But I smiled.

Getting warmer, Johnny.

Another door.

Warmer.

Another door.

Warmer!

The last door.

Hot!

I didn't open it at first. I just stared it down, relishing that split second before I met her, and knife met flesh. Blood was coming. My hand reached to open the door.

Slowly now, boy. Slowly.

Screeeeech.

I pushed the door open. I licked my lips, knife gripped at the ready. What little light there was showered into the stall.

It was empty.

Damn it!

Damn, I thought. But I didn't have much time to think before I heard, "Hey you!"

I turned around to find the girl. A warped and beat up broomstick lay in both her hands, pushed out in front of her like a shield. I smiled.

Like that will help.

I took a step closer to her, knife out before me.

Two can play that game.

She screamed, like a feral cat, but it was hardly a deterrent. Her face filled with fear as I came still closer. She had expected me to be afraid, a girl with a weapon and a mouth was to be feared. She had expected me to find her and had already planned for her glorious mastery over this monster.

Not you. Not this time.

Not me, Hyde, not this trip around the sun.

I stepped toward her, knife at my side. Not pointed at her, just resting at the ready. She whimpered and cried, holding her pathetic weapon in front of her. Despite the fight in her, she let me walk straight up to her. Close, closer, close enough to touch her.

I gently pulled the hair away from her face. I caressed it in my fingers. Gently. Softly. When her guard fell just a little, I yanked it—*hard.* She screamed. I smiled. She trembled with fear as she cried out. I soaked it in as if she were calling my name in passion. It was intoxicating. I had a firm grip on her. She didn't move anymore, except for her damn shaking. I leaned into her, my body pressing against hers, pressing her against the wall polluted with perverse graffiti. I rather liked the idea of killing her against the backdrop of other people's loud and obtrusive anger.

I breathed her in, stink and all. Her in my grasp with the knife in my hand, felt so good.

Hyde was oh, so very happy. I sank deeper into my brain, letting him come to the surface. From my sanitary waiting room, I watched as he plunged the knife into her bony flesh with a viscous crunch. He ground it deep inside. Again, and again, and again. Blood, all was blood then. Flowing freely. I was flowing with it, bursting open like a frozen river in the tides of early spring.

She screamed at first. A blood-curdling scream that gurgled up from the bottom of her throat as it filled with blood and vomit. Then, there was only silence. It was the silence that woke me. Startled me up from the back of my brain to the surface again just in time to see the carnage.

Her body was a beautiful mess. Splayed out like a deer carcass being processed after a long, exhausting hunt. I felt the breathless aftermath, the wake of passion and delight that remained. The knife was still in my hand, thickly veiled in blood, hair, and tissue. All of it dripping steadily to the ground. I could barely distinguish her face and figure in that mess. I realized I was standing in her blood, which pooled on the filthy bathroom floor. It was so thick that even my socks were wet with it.

I listened for the noise, the drumming sound of Hyde in my head to tell me what to do. He was sated, and he had gone to sleep it off. I felt sort-of alone. Alone with his mess that I had to clean up. But it was my mess too, and something had to be done about it.

I sighed as I grabbed some paper towels from the broken dispenser. I washed and dried my knife with the precision of a doctor caring for his instruments. After all, this was my craft. My one talent. My world.

I slammed my truck door shut and sat there, gripping the steering wheel loosely. I sat there in a daze, drunk on the blood and the danger and the sweet, sweet smell of death that clung to my clothes, and my skin.

My clothes.

I was covered in bloody spatter. Glancing in the rear-view mirror, I saw my face was also painted in blood that carved out a cruel, hungry smile at the corners of my lips. I tried to wipe it away, but it only smeared. Well—that wouldn't do. I heard low grumbling laughter in the hollow of my mind.

Stupid boy. You missed a spot.

I washed off my face in the restroom sink. I decided to change my clothes right there by the truck. I found my bag of clothes and stripped off everything there in the parking lot. It was dark out now and no one had driven down that road in more than an hour. I threw my bloodied clothes in the bottom of my bag and got back into the driver's seat.

I sat in the darkness, replaying everything, savoring every moment. Every delectable bite. In the dark of the night, it felt like I was watching my favorite movie; an old familiar friend I often sat down to visit. When it was over, I smiled.

"Welcome home, Johnny."

5 STRAWBERRIES AND CHAMPAGNE TO MY BLOOD AND BONES (OR #5)

My new apartment was small, even smaller than my last one, and that was *small*. I couldn't fit a bed in the little nook between the kitchenette and the bathroom that they called a bedroom. So, I bought an old, well-used futon and stuck it there. Livingroom/Bedroom/Love shack—yeah, that's what I labeled it.

I didn't use the kitchenette. I didn't know how to do anything but microwave hot dogs. You can get pretty sick of hot dogs. So, I ate out a lot. Whatever I could afford, mostly Chinese. I liked the number eleven combo platter at the China Dragon just down the street. They knew me well there and would always give me an extra eggroll and fortune cookie. I stuck the fortunes on the wall.

Every day was the same. Wake up. Work. Dinner. Sleep. Repeat. I skipped the bar these days. I wanted my mind always at the ready. The alcohol just slowed me down. I attributed my excessive use of it before to my failure at my secret pleasure. If I had only kept my guard up, kept myself vigilant, I could have done more, maybe even found Her.

The past is the past. I couldn't look back now with disappointment and regret. I just had to move forward. This was a new city after all. A new start. A new everything.

I wasn't one for decorating. I thought the half-empty Chinese takeout boxes and plastic milk jugs gave it a little character, made it mine. The walls were yellowed, stained by years of smokers. I got tired of staring at them, so eventually I tacked a poster of a famous painting on the ceiling above my futon bed. I would look at it in the night, daydreaming in its vibrant swirl of happy colors. It calmed the fury of my mind on nights when there was no quiet in there. I liked that picture.

I didn't sleep much. The neighbors were too loud. Yelling, screaming, pounding, crying babies, and barking dogs kept me up. I would have stayed in bed all day to make up for it, but there was work on weekdays. So, every day at five in the morning, regardless of whether my eyes had even closed, I rolled out of my bed, tossed my ass into the shower, and threw on some clothes. Then I grabbed an eggroll out of the fridge and headed off.

This particular morning, I hadn't slept a wink. When five o'clock rolled around, my eyes were already open, staring at my picture of paradise. Lost in it. I glanced over at the electric clock on my coffee table. Time to get up.

The water came out in a dribble from the clogged showerhead. I always meant to fix it, but I never seemed to find the time. I stood under it anyway and let it spit out rusty water on my dirty skin, hoping it would wash away the boredom and the angst crawling underneath.

I dunked my head under the showerhead. As the water came down, I was baptized in the silence. In the quiet, my mind was content and still.

Well, well. Isn't it quiet?

My eyes shot open like I was waking from the dead. It had been weeks since I had heard that old familiar voice that, at once frightened me and made me warm with pleasure. I smiled out of politeness, as if the thing inside of me could see it. I forgot the shower, the water spitting in my eyes as it turned from tepid to stone cold. I forgot everything and I listened.

The room got very, very quiet. I was focused. So focused that I imagined the drops of water above me had slowed to a stop and froze there in the air before my eyes. My breaths came steady, heavy, and loud.

Did you miss me? Tell me you missed me.

I was still running off the high from the gas station girl. I wasn't ready for another. How the hell could he be hungry again? I had filled him full and to the brim. Satiated his every wicked whim and desire carving that girl into a thousand pieces for his pleasure. Now, he wanted more?

Always.

I shut the water off. The pipes inside the walls groaned and whined. I stood naked in the small tub, dripping dry. My skin erupted in tiny goose pimples, and a shiver went down my spine. I didn't know why I was suddenly terrified. I wasn't afraid of Hyde. Nor of his delicately balanced hand on the switch inside my brain. But in that moment, I was afraid. It felt like something between impending doom and nausea. A globulus knot in the pit of my stomach, dead set on erupting. Filling me with dread and stomach acid. A revolt of all my senses, my whole body, at the thought of—what? I was afraid to answer that.

***

A girl at my job asked me out. I said no. She wasn't pretty. She wasn't smart. She could be a distraction from the voice of Hyde. He constantly played like a monotonous record on loop in my head.

Walking down the street.

Look, boy. Look at that one. Lovely, don't you think?

In the grocery store.

You know what you're hungry for, Johnny.

Alone.

Can't we get out of here and go play!

I was avoiding the me inside. The voracious appetite and cocky attitude were starting to frustrate me. It was never-ending. The urge was getting stronger and harder to stave off. I would have to do something about it soon, but I wasn't ready.

The girl at my job asked me out again. This time I said yes. She insisted on picking me up. She was late. Her tiny yellow and black Prius buzzed down my street like a horny little bumble bee. She called it the "Mancatcher." I couldn't imagine why. It was anything but attractive. It was a little sad, just like her.

She wouldn't tell me where we were going, only that it was a surprise. I didn't much care for surprises, and I was picky about my food. I was grateful she gabbed on the entire ride. It helped shut up the mindless chatter in my head.

"You know what I mean?" Her nasal, high-pitched voice broke into my noise, and I turned to see her looking at me with a smile.

Her eyes weren't on the road, not even a little, and her head was cocked obnoxiously to the side, like she was trying to be coy. Flirty. Cute.

Ugh.

I stumbled a bit and mumbled, "Yeah."

I had no idea what the hell she had been talking about, but my stunted answer was enough for her. She smiled and finally moved her eyes back to the road. I sighed with relief a little too loud in the silence that ensued. It was almost eerily quiet. So much so that I finally glanced over to her.

She was tense, I could tell. She gripped the pink fluffy steering wheel cover tightly. A smile was plastered on her face, though I could tell she was anything but happy. She was nervous—terribly, terribly nervous. She took a deep breath and slowly let it out. Her lips were trembling. It made me wonder where she was taking me.

Suddenly, the car stopped, and she turned to me

with that fake smile. I looked around, noticing we were in a dodgy neighborhood. Dodgier than mine. It was a part of the city I hadn't been in yet. I had been a bit lazy since I got into town. I didn't venture further than the few blocks from my apartment.

"Where are we?" I asked quietly.

Her smile got a little wobbly, but wider. She batted her eyes, though they didn't look straight at me. "My apartment."

She waited, as if this was some big reveal, a naughty transgression on her own part that she was confessing not to what she had done, but what she intended to do.

I reeled inwardly at the idea she seemed to have in mind for us this evening. I wasn't stupid. She was the company frump girl, one that was willing to pay for a good time because she couldn't get it any other way. In other words, she was renting me for the night. She had the wheel, the controls, everything. She was going to tell me how this was going to go. By saying yes, I had signed away any rights I had to the evening's goings-on. Alright, maybe this time, *I* had been a little stupid.

There was no way to get out of it. She was my only ride home and I had promised myself I would be good tonight.

"Alright," I said.

Her face lit up like a Christmas tree, all sparkly and bright with the hope of what was to come. She opened her door and wiggled out with delight. Slam! Her door shut.

I took a minute to get out. I really didn't want to sleep with her. Didn't want to even touch her, let alone kiss that gabby, cottonmouth of hers. Maybe after dinner, I could fake food poisoning or something. Maybe. I saw her standing on the sidewalk, anxiously smiling back at me, and gesturing me to come. I got out of the car and followed her.

Up four flights of dark stairs and down a narrow

hallway with rows and rows of red-painted doors. I glanced at the numbers on the door, 423, 433, 439, 444. We stopped there at 444. She turned to me with a flip of her fat, greasy hair.

"Neat, isn't it? The number? I'd like to think that it's my guardian angel watching over me. Keeping me safe from all those serial killers and monsters out there." She giggled as she finished speaking. I laughed too, but not for the same reason.

She unlocked the door, taking her time. Her hands were shaking, though I know she'd done this a hundred times with a hundred different men. Some she knew. Some she wanted to and some she just didn't care about. Oh yeah, I had heard the stories.

The door swung slowly open, and she motioned me inside first. Politely, I squeezed past her chubby figure to get inside. I heard her breathe in deeply as my body pressed up against hers. She liked it; I didn't. Her body was nothing but fluff and fat. I could feel it like gelatin in a mold, wriggling to get out of that tight body shapewear she must have stuffed herself into for this "date." I tried not to cringe and slid past her.

She held her breath as we had touched, but now it came tumbling out like a stunted waterfall or a dam that had burst. She hid it with another spurt of giggling as she came in and closed the door. I stood in her living room, looking around, taking things in.

It wasn't bad; better than mine. Despite the crappy apartment, she had done a good job of making it look like a home. It was an explosion of floral prints, all different, but somehow, they all seemed to go together. There was potpourri in shiny, decorative bowls everywhere I looked. Probably to drown out the hint of marijuana I smelled coming from the neighbors to the right of her apartment. Fresh flowers decorated the coffee table and the island in the kitchenette. They were just carnations. They were probably all she could afford, but they helped make the place seem alive.

I sat down gingerly on the sofa, invaded with dozens of tiny, overstuffed pillows, also, floral. She sat down next to me. Close, very close to me. So close, I imagined she could see the sweat beading on my upper lip. It was rather warm in here. Or maybe it was just me.

She motioned to the coffee table, and it was then that I saw what she was after. Chocolate-covered strawberries and a bottle of champagne. Two water-spotted champagne flutes. Flower petals scattered across the smudged glass surface of the table.

Looking very pleased with herself, she popped the cork on the champagne bottle with an obnoxious little squeal that sounded like a pig being slaughtered. She waited for the fizz to run out, making a wet spot on the beige shag carpet, and then she poured us both a glass. She handed a glass to me with an unsubtle smile.

"Drink up!" She said softly. Now I really knew what she wanted. The champagne was disgustingly warm. I didn't finish it, placing it half-drunk on the coffee table. The girl looked disappointed, her pursed and chubby cherub face giving me an ugly pout. That probably got her what she wanted with other guys. They probably did whatever she asked just to mask that awful face with a plastic smile, so they wouldn't have to look at it. I wasn't that desperate or that stupid. So, I sat and smiled back with my own dumb look.

The girl looked disappointed, but I didn't care. My head was throbbing something awful. It was filled to the brim with the voice of Hyde. No matter how much I tried to put a damper on his slick, coaxing voice, he was persistent. Babbling until his words were a thick cloud of nonsense fogging up my brain.

The girl was just as persistent. She threw back her glass of champagne in one gulp and set down her glass. Before I knew it, she was leaning into me, her body heat and cheap perfume making me dizzy and sick. Her face was caked with heavy makeup and overdone. It wasn't the right shade either and it gave her an orange-tint. That's what she was: a plump, over-ripe orange, rolling into me on this disgusting secondhand couch permeated with secondhand smoke. Now I really was sick. I could feel the acid in my stomach churning fast and rising into my throat.

And then, it just all came up. On her, on me, on her ugly freaking floral couch. I didn't apologize. I didn't say anything. I just threw up again. She was beyond disgusted, nearly gagging herself.

"What the hell, Johnny?" She exclaimed, jumping up from the couch.

Of course, when she did that, my puke slid onto the floor. That was evidently too much for her. Her hand clamped on her mouth, and she ran from the room.

Good boy.

I couldn't help but smile with Hyde on that one. I certainly saved myself there.

Now, can we get on with it?

Hyde laughed; I laughed. I could hear her throwing up her warm champagne and cheap ass chocolate-covered strawberries. That was enough for me. She wasn't one of the lovelies, not by a long shot, but she was a wily rung on the ladder toward Her. One that had to be conquered and cleared away before I could reach the ultimate in perfection. The *One.* So—

Take her.

Alright, I will.

By the time she had enough gumption to come out of the bathroom, I had been waiting just outside for quite a while, brandishing a nice shiny meat cleaver. I had found it while milling around her apartment. She didn't see me in the shadows, so it was easy to sneak up on her.

Pop!

One blow to the head and she was out like a light. A very large, orange, persistent and rather annoying light, which I took the liberty of smashing into a billion little bits. It was a glorious mess. When I was done, I stood over what was left of her, breathless and victorious. But, not satisfied. My body had complied, but my heart hadn't been in it. I knew I didn't want a taste of such bitter, over-ripe fruit that was already rotting. However, Hyde had been insistent.

Feverish, my stomach still churning angrily, I left the rubble and the ruin behind, after clearing the space of any trace of me. Except, that is for the mess. I left. Why bother? I wasn't worried about being caught. There was too long a list of men that would better fit the role of suspect than me. After all, I was invisible, remember?

I stumbled into her pink—very pink—bathroom and stepped into the shower, clothes, and shoes still on. I blasted the hot water on myself, washing away the blood, the puke and the mess. I looked for Hyde within the confines of my brain, but he was nowhere to be found. He was full and happy now.

6 Raw

My clothes were still soaking wet as I walked the last mile and a half back to my apartment., Despite the busy traffic, no one seemed to notice me. I could hear my socks squishing in my shoes over the honking, cars, and the sounds of the streets. It was dark by the time I got home. Me covered in puke and blood, before soaking myself in that girl's shower until it ran down the drain, along with remnants of her, was not how I had expected the evening to go.

I was, stranded on a Friday night, hungry and still feeling a little sick. The shower had helped with the feverish feeling a little, but now, despite the heat of the night, I shivered uncontrollably. I wrapped my arms around myself, but nothing helped.

"Hey!" I heard a woman's voice calling from behind me.

The sound of an engine and the crunching of gravel followed, as a car steadily approached me. In a daze, I turned around to find a truck, older and junkier than mine with a young woman in the driver's seat. The light was on in her truck, and I could see her peering out at me with a look of genuine concern. She was beautiful. A halo of yellow light crowning her head made her look like an angel. In that moment, still feverish and weak, she was an angel to me.

She pulled up next to me, rolling down the passenger side window to yell out, "Come on in, honey. Looks like you need a ride."

That was it, all I needed was an invitation. I climbed into her truck in a matter of seconds not bothering with the seatbelt. In a flash, we were rolling into traffic. It was quiet for several minutes, but her eyes kept sidling to me, checking me over.

I knew she didn't want me—not like that. I could see the kindness in her dark blue eyes and a sense of relief washed over me. Hyde was quiet. If not satisfied, at least silenced for the moment. My head was pounding, and my stomach was lurching again, ready to purge whatever remnants of my date there were left. I kept the window rolled down just in case.

"You gotta name, honey?" she asked softly over the noise of the truck.

I was barely conscious then. Barely alive, it felt like. If only my head would stop pounding.

"Johnny, be good," I mumbled in my fever dream.

"Johnny? Is that your name?" the young woman said.

I wasn't good for an answer. I felt myself slip into a cool, quiet darkness and that was all I remembered.

I was dreaming. I knew I had to be dreaming because my mother was there. In real life, my mother was dead. Gone for at least ten years. Most of my memories of her had long since faded and disappeared. But there she was, slipping into my dark like a fragrant, easy shadow.

I saw her there, sitting at the old, rusted kitchen table in the house on Walnut Street. She was wearing her old threadbare blue dress. A crossword puzzle sat abandoned beneath her hand that rested on the table. She was looking straight at me, her eyes full of tears, and her lips slowly wobbling.

"Johnny," she said, and her voice was all echoes like a dream sequence in a movie. "Johnny, be good."

She pounded her fist on the table. It quaked and rattled beneath the force of her small hand.

"Why can't you be good?"

I heard myself answer. "I'm always good, Mama.

For you, always."

She shook her head violently, her tears falling now like water breaking through a dam, a levy destroyed and flood waters rising.

"Don't!" she cried. "You lie too much."

"When have I lied to you, Mama?"

Her eyes narrowed. "Not to me, to yourself."

Like a shadow, her old body shifted at lightning speed. Suddenly, she was in front of me, staring me down. She was breathing me in and out, as if my trembling fear gave her body and life.

"You let him run wild in there, spoiling your beautiful mind and rotting all your insides," my mother exclaimed.

I could see the palsies in her hands running wild, her body all aquiver.

"You're rotten, Johnny. Rotten to the core. Rotten, way down deep, and there's no getting out of the hole you've dug for yourself. Just you wait, Johnny. Just you wait. The blood and the death and the evil will catch up with you. It will catch up with you!"

It will catch up with you. The words kept screaming in my aching head, escaping in the darkness there as my mama's bent and crooked figure vanished in a tunnel of shadows. The memory and my mama faded. And then all there was left was darkness. Deep and deathly silent.

Slowly, the sound of my own breathing filled the silence. It was steady, constant, and deep. I relished my consciousness in the dark, able to listen to my surroundings without the burden of looking. I could feel my body begin to move and flex. I felt my limbs stretching and a wave of cold that seemed to waft up onto every inch of me. Despite the cold, it was peaceful. And then—

"You alright, honey?"

My eyes shot open, my head instantly aching. I

blinked in the bright light gleaming through the open blinds over the nearby window. The light was so damn bright. I groaned and turned away from it. Sitting up, I realized I was on a beat-up old couch. There were cigarette burns on the arms and the stuffing was tumbling out of the holes. Nonetheless, it was comfortable.

I remembered someone asking me a question.

"What?" I muttered, peering around the room to see who had spoken.

I found the young woman. She wasn't that young, now that I got a good look at her. She was sitting on the edge of the coffee table next to me. In the light, I could see the harsh lines on her face, along her eyes and next to her lips, that took the edge off her beauty. She wasn't as lovely in the light of day. She looked down on me with a worn smile, one she must use for everyone she met. It was still nice and a bit comforting. I sat up fully, the couch springs squeaking under me.

"You alright?" she asked again.

I took her in for a minute, the illusion of her beauty quickly fading. Gently, she leaned into me and wiped away a stain of wetness under my eyes.

"You were crying in your sleep," she whispered, as if, were she to say it any louder, I might burst into more tears out of shame.

I hadn't noticed the tears still running down my face until then. Quickly, I pulled away from her touch and wiped off all evidence of them myself. She wasn't offended. She just smiled that worn and weary smile with a sigh. Her bare shoulders sagged like she carried the weight of the world on them.

Her white tank top was spotless, her rather diminutive chest barely making waves in it. She was skinny, like poor skinny, which would explain the ratty couch, and from the looks of it, the grim and musty apartment. From the dusty knick-knacks and dying flowers on the kitchen table, I could see that she cared enough to try and make it nice. Things must have always gotten in the way. Too many people to take care of. Too much work to be done.

She saw me looking around and smiling.

"Sorry about the mess. My husband's away for a couple weeks. He's a trucker, you know? Always away. When he's gone, I tend to just let things slip a little. Don't have the heart to keep up with it all. I miss him, you know? But, boy, I'll have my hands full cleaning in a couple days. That's when he comes back."

She shut up then, realizing I was not ready for girly gabbing. She handed me a glass of water. I grabbed it from her, tossing it back like a shot, drinking it down in one long gulp.

"Easy, kid. You don't want it coming back up," said the woman.

She was right. My stomach cramped and I felt the water chug and churn its way down, fighting all the way. I swallowed hard. The water stayed down. I handed her back the glass. Shivering in the cold, I realized I was all but naked underneath the quilt she had given me. It wore years of stains, its colorful pattern faded, the fabric and fluff chewed up and frayed.

"My clothes," I muttered low.

She stood up, disappearing into what must have been her bedroom. She came back out with my clothes, neatly folded and dry. She stood over me and handed them to me.

"There you go, kid. Clean, dry, and folded. I even got the puke stains out for you. Took a little scrubbing." She smiled softly, proud of herself.

She left me then. Turned her back and busied herself in the kitchen. I slipped out of the comfort of the quilt. Standing naked in the middle of the room. I stumbled back into my clothes, struggling to focus my eyes to tie both my shoes. I still felt a bit woozy and a bit empty too. My stomach growled low and loud at me. My head began to spin, and I tumbled back down on the couch, resting it between my knees.

The woman sensing that she had an audience began to talk as she worked to tidy up the tiny space.

"It's funny, when my husband's here, there aren't enough hours in the day. Time just speeds by, like lightning in a bottle if you're fast enough to catch it. You have to hold onto every second so you can remember everything in the bad times. Every good moment that's special. Because the second they're gone, that's it. That's all you have.

"Sometimes I lie awake at night, just lie there, watching him sleep. And I realize that everything beautiful and lovely is right there. It's sort of an overwhelming feeling when you find the one. It's just like—the sun and the moon and the galaxies and the whole damn universe all collided so that these two people, these two souls can meet. You know?"

I didn't know. And I didn't care. I was long gone before she could finish. I don't know if her husband really was on his way back. Or if he ever got there to meet her and satisfy her love, which seemed all-consuming. Maybe she was just as lost as I was and told herself the same story every day to keep it real. Either way, it didn't matter. Not to me.

***

Home. Closed blinds. Darkness.

I slept deep and long for what seemed like forever. But the sleep was restless and full of dreams. Dreams like memories that crept up quietly and clamped down on my subconscious, until I felt like I would burst. Instead, I awoke in tears, screaming my lungs out. The sound of my own voice screeching like a banshee, terrified me.

It was dark now, a cool breeze drifting in from the

broken window. I watched the faded curtains sway in the wind for a minute, listening to the hiss of the fabric as it moved. The noise of traffic leaked in from the street as did the rolling rumble of distant thunder. Despite this ambient noise, the air was still. The quiet was deep. I sighed letting the tear stains dry on my cheeks.

My mind was clear now, keenly clear and alert, as if it had been asleep for a long, long while and finally woken up. Hyde was nowhere to be found in that mass of nerves and tissues. For the first time, I was glad. I was getting tired of his constant barrage of insults and demands. Always beating me. Always stretching my nerves until I almost broken and beating my brain into a pulp like he owned it.

Five. It was Five now and I was sick to death of the whole thing. It churned my stomach raw to think of the terrible things I had done. Things that would gut-punch any normal human being into oblivion with fear and guilt. I had never felt those things before. But here in the quiet of the night, they came for me. They crept into my conscience like a cold, wet blanket. One heavy and full of feelings I didn't want or understand. In all this, one word with a voice all its own, rose up.

Monster.

I'd never thought of myself as a monster. I never considered myself to be like everyone else. I was superior, but certainly not a monster. Now, that word, that voice of judgment, was all that I heard.

Monster. Monster. Monster.

It tumbled and tore through every inch of me, spreading like wildfire on a windy plain.

"Monster," I whispered.

Maybe it was true.

7 RAGE (OR...STARING AT THE DAMN HOLE IN THE WALL)

Cravings are funny things. They seem to come and go on their own time, at their own pace, and they usually don't listen to what you really want. Though, I suppose they are what you really want. They have their own voice, but it's really just yours—the real you, screaming out for what you can't live without. Always hungry. Always waiting for another divinely designed opportunity, which always seems to come when they need it most. Try as you might, you can't turn them off. You can't erase them or the need they present. So, you give up and listen. Listen until you can't tell where their voice ends and yours begins.

But I didn't want to listen—not so soon and not so fast. I felt my body slipping into a cavernous deep. I knew that once my head went under the murky darkness, I would never be able to come up again. Not as anything that I could recognize anyway. I wasn't ready to give in completely. I still wanted that piece of me that said, "I can do without this. It's just for fun."

Yet it was quickly becoming impossible to say that this was merely a recreation. It was becoming all-consuming. Something that I *needed*. It was a delicious need now; a wonderful and horrible addiction that was beginning to define my flesh and blood and bones.

And I liked it.

Well, part of me did. The other part was slow to accept this as my new normal. Crave, hunt, kill. Crave, hunt, kill. Repeat as desired. There was a sliver of my insides that was still terrified at the fact that I needed more. More than one. More than two. More and more and more and more to make me feel alive, satisfied, and whole. If you can feel whole picking up other people's rotten pieces for your own.

I didn't like how much I needed this. I drank myself into delirium to drown it all out, way down deep. Deeper than the feverish stupor I had been in not long ago, when I had made short work of my coworker. I barely remembered anything from that night or the days after. Whatever got hold of me held on tight. I was not even close to my right mind for a while.

I lay half on and half off my bare mattress, staring down a damn hole in the wall. The evidence from the night before when I had run out of beer. Didn't get out of bed. I didn't go out. I didn't see anyone. I didn't do anything. I just sat staring down that hole, while I felt like my brain was being lobotomized, piece by glorious piece. My memories and my plastic feelings were being dug through and put on display in search of anything that made me human. The voices in my head decided unanimously that there wasn't anything to be found there.

I was out of beer and out of my mind. My stomach was beyond empty and the hole in the wall was taunting me. Maybe it was the alcohol or lack thereof. Maybe it was whatever kind of sick I was, or maybe it really was, but as I stared down the hole, I watched the wall surrounding it begin to sliver and crack. Crumbling pieces of drywall tumbled to the floor and the hole grew bigger. Large enough for me to see something fluttering and moving on the other side. It was dark, just a shadow, but it made me sit up and stare. Something was watching me from that hole in the dark.

I cocked my head to the side, half-amused and

terrified. Despite my fear, I smiled at it, whatever it was. I pushed myself off the bed and edged closer to the wall. Standing in front of the crumbling wall, that hole seemed so much larger now than it had been a moment before. It was nearly the size of my face. The dark was deep inside of it, but there was something there that was deeper than the dark. A shape in the shadows that was staring back.

"Hello there," I said, cautious and low.

There was no answer. The shadow in the dark was small, now that I got a better look at it. Smaller than me, like a kid.

"What are you doing there in the dark?" I asked.

Still no answer. And then—

I heard a whisper in the dark. It crept through the plaster and wood like an echo in a tunnel. I couldn't understand what it said. Instinctively, I leaned in closer, my face just inside the cavernous hole. The whispered words just kept coming. It grew louder and louder, until the voice was screaming, high-pitched and childlike.

"Rotten!" it screamed in a voice that was strangely familiar.

The voice was like a memory that itched at the back of your brain, but you couldn't quite scratch its surface. I couldn't quite lift the veil of confusion to see it for what it was.

The sound of the scream blasted me backward onto the floor, startling me. My heart was beating so fast. I was breathless. I knew there was something there in that dark that I didn't want to see. But I looked anyway, catching a glimpse of a young face I knew well.

My own, as a child.

It was pale and dark-eyed. Frightened, which was my permanent expression, thanks to my mom.

Frightened me stared back at frightened me. I remembered all the dark things that I had hidden away in my childhood. Things adults did in the dark when you were small and helpless. The look in my mother's eyes; that look of guilt and resignation mixed into a numbed and tranquil smile. The images, the smells, the fear all came rushing back at me like a tidal wave. A tsunami of shit that I hadn't ever wanted to remember again.

It made me sick. So sick. I felt like it was pushing up and out of my body. I vomited there on the spot, letting out those fears and bad feelings. Purging them. But when I had emptied everything in my stomach, the feelings were still there inside.

"Rotten to the core. Johnny, be good."

The voice trailed off and disappeared. There wasn't a remnant or even an echo of it on the air. I scrambled off the floor and moved toward the wall. The hole was just a hole, small and barely noticeable, not the giant blackhole I had seen a minute before. There were no shadows. No me inside of it. It was just a hole.

Something trembled inside me, trembled, and shivered up from my empty, aching stomach working up through my throat until I felt it rising to my lips. I screamed until I couldn't scream anymore. And I punched the wall again. This time, I made a real hole. I felt something crack and crunch in my hand. Something had broken, I knew it.

Great, now there would be a hospital visit. Questions. Eyes. Eyes on me everywhere. I cussed under my breath as I turned my back on the hole I had made with the rage I had unearthed. It was here now, the rage. It was here to stay. It had probably always been there. And I knew the cravings and the urges were the only thing that would make it go away. It was the cure to my illness. The antidote to the poison running through my veins. It was everything.

***

I sat by myself behind the emergency room partition, waiting to be seen. My hand was propped up on a pillow and packed with ice. I had sobered up by now, but my head was rushing and throbbing like a freight train. My eyes looked like blood-stained saucers and my skin was deathly pale. I could see myself in the reflective metal of the supply cabinet next to me. I looked like that child version of me. Afraid and frantic. Like a deer in the headlights. I tried to water down the emotions spilling out on my face. I didn't want the doctor to get any ideas. No talk of voices. No talk of people in walls or mothers who touched you in funny places. No, none of that.

I closed my eyes, the sounds of the bustling emergency room streaming in toward me like a river current, ebbing and flowing in a steady rush of noise. The sounds of machines. People crying, screaming, puking. People's last words and last breaths mixed in with arguments and tears. I breathed it in like a tonic, relishing the chaos that made my own seem muted at least for the moment.

"...Daddy...don't listen to the doctor, you're fine...this is it, isn't it...please, please, she's suffering, please just give her the medicine...I need someone, a doctor, anyone, please...please, be good...Now to our next news story, the disturbing murder of Helena Briggs..."

My eyes shot open. The TV was on in the waiting area, and I could see it from where I sat if I squinted. But I didn't need to squint to see that girl from work. Her face, as big and ugly as ever was plastered all over the television screen. The news reporter went on and on about how tragic her death was and how horrific the crime scene had been. Blah, blah, blah. I was uninterested. That is, until they said they were on the hunt for her killer. They claimed they had evidence, and every day was one step closer to finding the son of a bitch. (I added the son of a bitch part. Of course, they wouldn't call a killer what he really was on national television.)

It felt less like a news report and more like the start of a witch hunt. And what was this evidence that they were bragging about? I had been careful. Well, I barely remembered that night. I *thought* I had been careful. I was always careful. But I had left an awfully beautiful mess behind me. I could have left something behind.

That wide-eyed look of terror filled my face again, just as the doctor strolled in to look at my arm. I said nothing but the basics. I answered his questions quietly and with little drama. Still, he watched me like a freaking hawk. Eyed my every move. My eye twitched a little and I swear I saw him huff with a judgmental and an accusatory sigh. He was watching me, alright.

The doctor smiled. His name was John according to his crisp white coat, but his name would just as quickly be forgotten in my muddled brain. Names meant nothing to me. People meant nothing to me.

"You broke your wrist pretty good there, John," the doctor said.

I looked at him. Just looked at him for a moment, trying to decide whether or not to answer. Finally—

"It's Johnny. John was my father."

"Mine too. But unfortunately for me, it's just John," the doctor smiled as he talked. That plastic commercial smile that he must have given everyone he'd seen that night. "Got a girl, Johnny?"

Do I have a girl? Well, Dr. John, I have five.

But instead, I said, "No. Don't have a girl."

Eyes down. Avoid his eyes.

"Do you get in fights a lot, Johnny?"

Why did he keep saying my freaking name?

"Nope, no fights. Just hit my damn hand on the damn wall. Oops, I guess."

He smiled, it was softer now and more personal. "I gotcha," he said.

I looked at him now. He was busy with my wrist and the cast, and not me. What was his angle? What was he getting at with all these stupid questions and small talk?

He looked like he wanted to say more, but instead, he just placidly smiled and patted me on the shoulder.

"All done," he said and was gone.

The nurse gave me a sideways glance and then she was gone too. I was free to go. I haven't high tailed it out of a place so fast in my life. My wrist was numb in the white cast they had put on me and the drugs they had given me were kicking in. No pain, but plenty of worries.

Had I been careful? *Had* I been careful? *Had I been careful?*

The question kept replaying in my aching head. I tried to play back that night, but the details were as fuzzy and blurry as my eyesight on this damn medicine. Damn it. I needed to think clearly now. I needed to think.

I passed a local bar and stopped at the entrance. I edged closer, just inside. Enough to see the beer on tap dripping from its foamy spout. The bar patrons— oh so happy with their alcoholic happiness in a glass— they were all sitting in the dim neon-lit splendor of carefree carelessness. I licked my lips. I needed something. Just a taste. Just a—

Before I knew it, I was sitting at the bar with a drink in my one good hand. One drink, two drinks, three drinks, four drinks, it didn't matter at this point. The world was spinning like crazy, and my stomach was empty and aching, but I just kept going. By the time I was done, I was swaying in my seat, trying to keep my head on straight enough to keep my butt plastered there. The bartender cut me off at that point, but he let me stay. He poured me a cup of black coffee, but I didn't touch it. Caffeine didn't do a thing for me, and it really wasn't going to help my nerves.

Then I heard it—that same damn news story about that girl. It was on the TV plastered to wall in the corner. Different news reporter this time. But the story was the same. She was killed. It was horrible. Searching for the killer. Blah, blah, blah, blah, blah. I was fading fast, but I caught the end of the story, the sappy part where the reporter expresses his personal opinion, a plea for help, something to hook the viewers and make them feel—something.

"...the community has been wracked with several of these horrendous murders and this most recent attack has brought it to its knees. We hope and pray that the killer will be found, and justice will be done."

I couldn't help but laugh out loud, catching the attention of some of the patrons sitting nearby. People just watched; they did nothing. I was okay though and I didn't notice much.

Yeah, go ahead and pray. Pray to whatever god you want, I'm not gonna stop. Not gonna stop hunting down your daughters, your sisters, your lovers, your friends. Not until I find what I'm looking for and I—

My thoughts seemed to stop, suddenly like a jolt of lightning to my over-medicated and over-stimulated brain. What would happen when I did find what I was looking for? *The One.* What would happen when I found Her? Was that it? Would the fun just stop? Would I even need it anymore?

The thought sent a shiver down my spine. The fact that stopping this blood fest frightened me only made me more frightened. If I wasn't going to be sated by finding my dream girl, would I ever be?

Whoa, whoa, whoa.

This was way too deep a conversation for the codeine concoction in my veins and the alcohol chaser I added to the mix. I was tripping and my brain was on fire. Instead of dwelling in that stupor of fear, I looked up at the television to see that stupid girl's face plastered all over the screen. Talk about an extreme close-up. She had always wanted everyone's attention. Well, now she had it. Not the kind of publicity she was hoping for, but still—attention was attention to those kind of people. I could bet you any amount of money that wherever she was rotting, she'd look up at that television and smile, like she was some kind of damn star.

I chuckled to myself, though it was a little loud, and I turned my eyes away from the TV screen. The bartender eyed me sharply, his expression an angry one.

"Hey, what's your problem, buddy?" he said with a certain air of toughness that didn't suit his diminutive size behind that bulky counter.

I laughed all the harder, flicking my cigarette ashes onto said counter, just to spite him.

I shook my head, muttering, "Nothing."

"What?" he said all the louder, blaring in my aching head.

I glared at him hard, slamming down my last drink. "I said nothing. Don't have a problem. Alright?"

He wasn't done.

"You think a girl getting murdered is funny, huh? What are you some kind of sicko or something that gets his kicks on stuff like that?"

More ashes on his dirty counter with a smirk on my drunken face.

"I'm sure she got what she wanted," I muttered, thinking no one would hear me. Not even that smug looking shorty tending the bar.

He must have heard me, because in a split second he was leaning over the bar and slugging me across the face. If I didn't already have a headache, I sure as hell had one now.

I slowly turned my head back to him. He was fuming, his chest heaving with his bottled-up anger. He didn't care who saw. He was going to kick my ass if I didn't leave. I tossed the remnants of my cigarette onto the bar.

Burn, baby, burn.

Holding up my hands in pathetic surrender, I sidled out of my seat and backed away from the bar. The man was still fuming, and he watched every step I made toward the door, until I was out.

The night was chilly and as soon as my skin hit the night air, it was on fire. Everything in my body ached and my head was woozy. I swayed on my feet, trying my best to stand still. I needed a minute to think. If I could think at all. I needed to find my way home if I was able. Home, I—

"What the hell am I doing here?" I whispered to the night, but the night didn't answer back. No one did.

8 #6, 7, 8 AND MY INABILITY TO CONTROL THE CRAVING

My rage didn't stop there. In fact, it fueled me to ramp up my search for that perfect girl. The perfect stain on my bloody map toward euphoria. Total and complete satisfaction. I was getting closer; I could feel it. Every body was a hop, skip and a jump closer toward my dream. And what a deliciously wonderful ride it was.

#6

Bubbles, bubbles, and a little bloody, bubbly fun. She wanted a hot date and a little TLC afterward. The bubble bath and champagne in cheap plastic glasses was her idea. I went along with it. I slipped into her rust-ringed clawfoot tub in scorching hot water with about a foot of bubbles frothing into my nether regions. A game of footsy, a bit of cuddling, and a few glasses of her mediocre champagne, and I was the only thing keeping her head above water. She was literal putty in my hands, moldable and easy to manipulate.

Slip, drip, slice!

The thing I liked about #6 was that she had a bit of a knife fetish. She collected them, every size, shape, and design. For me, it was like walking into a freaking candy store. When it came time for the big show, I could take my pick. I almost couldn't decide, while she lay indisposed on the couch, calling for me in her drunken stupor.

I finally decided on the karambit she had displayed on the mantle. It was a beauty. I had never seen anything like it in person, but I certainly knew what it was. She had pointed it out and shown it off when we took the little tour of her place. It was her prized possession, a real antique. I figured it was only right to use this for our playtime.

I wanted to relish the moment. But the knife was so pretty, so sharp and tantalizing. I just wanted to slice and dice my way through her. One swipe with that sexy curved blade and she was done. Goodbye, bubble girl. After that, I think I used every blade she had in the house. Trying them out to sample my kill. A light and deliciously clean feast for the eyes, the hands, the tongue, and every part of me.

#7

Hyde was living his best life when I found this one. It was like a movie. A dark and stormy night, and I was walking home in the rain. Out of the fog and the glow of the streetlights, there came this girl. She was young, very young, just barely old enough to be out late. Her see-through raincoat showed off her hot pink midriff shirt and those hips. She was built for a good time. It didn't take me long to peg her as the next one.

She saw me from a distance and smiled. The smile was sweet and not so innocent that I didn't know what it meant. She had *me* pegged as her next good time. She walked right past me, hips swinging beautifully, and I thought I had lost her. My heart nearly skipped a beat when she glanced back at me, her long blonde hair flipping back behind her as her smile grew wider. It was an invitation.

I gladly accepted and turned around to follow her. We ended up in her car, fogging up the windows with our midnight passion. It was nothing fancy and nothing great, but my lucky push dagger made quick work of my mediocre midnight lover. The mess afterward was something else. I was more careful now and left no trace of me ever being in that little sedan with the fog-patched windows. And if I was lucky that fog would hold out until morning. What a nice reveal that would be for all those early risers and morning joggers. Too bad I wasn't there to see it. I have to say it was some of my best work.

#8

Ugh. A waste of my time, really. What a mess. Who knew that something so thin and fragile could bleed so much. Now, blood for me is as intoxicating as wine, but this—this was just too much. And it wouldn't stop. One quick slice unleashed a tsunami of red, and it went everywhere.

I made the mistake of bringing her back to my apartment for the fun. I could have kicked myself at the stains on my carpet. It took hours to get it looking even remotely okay. Even when I was done with every bottle of bleach the local convenience store had, there was still a hint of brownish-yellow left where her body had landed. I dragged the coffee table over it. It actually looked a lot better there. Problem solved.

Only my problem wasn't really solved. I was a killing machine with no end in sight. I was quickly losing direction and focus. I was losing my dream of *Her* for a new dream filled with blood, flesh, and bone. All for the freaking fun of it.

That wasn't how it was supposed to be. It wasn't supposed to be just about the killing, the taste of sweet red. It was supposed to be about the ideal. The dream, the holy grail of women that when captured in the wild would release me from this stain, this curse, this burden of blood. But here I was, enjoying every damn minute of exactly what it wasn't about, until I forgot everything but the red.

It was after #8 that my cocky ass made a huge mistake. As if #5 wasn't enough of a mistake that I still had to keep tabs on, the almost #9 was just plain stupid on my part. I carpooled one night with a few people from work. They of course wanted to stop at a restaurant after our shift. I would have rather gone home to drink myself to oblivion and sleep, but I was stuck.

We ended up at a restaurant on the other end of town. A diner that didn't know whether it was a classic diner or a Mexican taco shack. Either way, the food wasn't bad. Not my thing (I hated Mexican food), but it wasn't the worse thing I'd eaten, and I was really hungry.

I was with two guys and two girls. I know, I know, it seems like double date material with Johnny as the fifth wheel. I couldn't stand the girls' high-pitched chatter and the guys' brainless guffawing, so I tuned them out. I started thinking about—well, to be honest, I wasn't really thinking about anything. I just wanted to shut out the noise. The restaurant was way too loud, too many people, and there was too much background noise in my already cluttered brain.

"Isn't that right, Johnny?"

The one guy—Dan, I think—was staring at me, waiting with a stupid grin on his face for my answer. I had no idea what they had been talking about and I guess it showed on my face, because Dan started to laugh, obnoxious, loud laughing. I could see other diners beginning to stare our way out of the corner of my eye.

Come on, Johnny. Play along.

So, I did. I laughed along with him.

He decided to repeat whatever he had said. "I bet Johnny's rolling in the ladies, huh? Isn't that right, Johnny?"

My laughter turned to a muffled chuckle. I wasn't amused. But Dan wasn't done. Damn it.

"Well, I don't know about that," I muttered, fiddling with the dirty fork that dangled off the edge of my plate.

Dan released his hungry hold on the girl sitting next to him and leaned over the table with a wide smile.

"That's not what I hear," he said. "I've heard about you. You run through girls like beer through a pisser."

A shiver ran up my spine. That sick feeling again, the acid and those disgusting tacos crawling back up my throat. My smile dropped off my face.

"Where'd you hear that?"

Dan smiled smugly, pleased with himself that he had the scoop on me. Or so he thought.

"Word gets around," said Dan. "It's not so big a city that everybody doesn't know everybody else's business, if you know what I mean." Dan whispered rather obnoxiously loud, so that the girls would hear, "You must love 'em hard too. The word around is that you're never seen with the same one twice. That's some loving, my friend."

I fidgeted uncomfortably in my seat. I could feel the sweat beading on my face, cool and damp, as I shivered all the harder.

"Is that true, Johnny?" one of the girls asked.

The look on her face was one of disgust and a little bit of fear, as if I was so damn obsessed with girls that I was gonna jump her right then and there. That would have made me laugh, were I not terrified myself.

Play it cool, Johnny. Play it cool. It's all just a game.

I put on a plastic smile for everyone around the table. One that said, "Go ahead, keep going, it's really amusing".

"I don't kiss and tell," I said with that stupid grin on my face. Just like magic, my body played along with the ruse, and I felt my cheeks burn hot. I saw them look at me with what looked like secondhand embarrassment.

Poor Johnny, his guts spilled out on the table for all to see.

Secrets divulged. Johnny exposed...so they might think.

There was some strained laughter and the conversation moved on to something else.

I turned my eyes away from my table to look around the diner, while my workmates' conversation drifted out of my consciousness again. It sounded more like a watery echo in my brain and the sounds of the diner took front and center. They were loud, panging in my ears like the sick ache of too much wine. I winced.

Then I heard it—that laughter—*Her* laughter. Like the sweet sounds of summer in the dead rage of winter. I turned toward the sound, and there she was. She was one of the waitresses, unfortunately not ours. She was standing behind the counter, talking to the line cook through the shuttered partition that separated the front of the diner from the kitchen. Her laugh was intoxicating.

I knew I was staring, but I didn't care. She was something to look at; a sweet, sweet flower amid a pile of weeds. She was short—let's just call her beautifully petite. A perfect little package wrapped up in a bow just for me. She was the perfect size and shape. I could tell even through her baggy white shirt, black stirrup leggings, and oversized red apron. Her hourglass shape, perfect complexion starred with a few freckles around her cheeks, and long straight auburn hair pulled back in a ponytail set me afire.

God, I wanted her. Wanted her for myself. The craving hit my gut like a bullet. Like a man possessed, I was up from my seat, walking away from the table.

"Hey, Johnny! Where ya going?" Dan called after me.

Reluctantly, I turned back to him, a sly smile spreading wildly across my lips.

"Got my wild oats to sow, if you know what I mean," I said.

Dan looked surprised. He gave me a wink and a smile, with a nod of approval. The girls at the table looked disgusted and turned away from me. Dan's attention quickly turned back to them. He was monopolizing the table, the attention, and the other guy (I don't really remember his name and never could) didn't have a chance. I was glad of that. They wouldn't notice I was missing.

I turned back to the counter, only to find the waitress was gone. My smile faded.

Damn it, Dan. You made me lose my focus and my fun for the night.

"Can I get you anything, sir?"

I turned around to see the girl right in front of me, her smile big and pleasing. She was ready to please me. Give me whatever I wanted. I could feel it.

"Your number?" I said, turning on the charm.

She giggled and her ponytail swung delightfully behind her. It was hypnotic. Her eyes sparkled like diamonds in the harsh fluorescent lighting of the diner. It was magical. I was so distracted I almost forgot what I had asked for.

She cocked her head to the side with a coy smile that appeared, at once, both hungry and shy. She looked like she didn't know whether to be flattered or shocked. That was alright, I would take either, as long as I got her in the end.

"You're pretty bold, aren't you—"

"Johnny," I filled in.

"Johnny," she repeated. The familiar ring of my own name sounded so much better on her glossy cherry-red lips. I could almost taste them.

Getting ahead of yourself, aren't you, Johnny?

Right. My brain and my body were always two steps ahead. I cleared my throat and smiled bashfully. All for show, but still, it was a good one. It got her attention. She probably thought I was cute, charming even in a shy sort of way. Something she could wrap her arms around by the way she looked at me.

"Well, Johnny," she started, blushing herself. "How about we start with coffee after my shift?"

Ugh. Great. She wasn't a mover and shaker; she was a talker. She wanted emotional intimacy and compatibility before she'd ever consider anything physical. I'd have to move heaven and earth then to get her to follow me home.

"Hello?"

Her voice broke my train of thought. "Sure, coffee sounds great," I choked out with a half-hearted smile.

She was pretty, but she definitely wasn't worth the hours of mindless gabbing and flirting that I was in for that evening. My heart sank. This was going to be a long night.

She smiled back whole-heartedly.

"I get off in twenty minutes," she said and then she was gone with a skip in her step and her ponytail swinging.

It was far less tantalizing now. I was already not in this for the right reasons, and rage was starting to get the better of me. I didn't want to wait for her. I didn't want to playact and play coy when all I wanted was to kill her. This wasn't going to be easy. She seemed wholesome and good, which meant it was going to be a slow ride to the kind of fun I wanted.

But, stupid me, I waited for her, my anger building with every passing second. I sat at the counter, for what seemed like an eternity, slowly falling into my own empty abyss until the sounds around me disappeared. I was preparing for the big show. The big fun. My body was already itching to get started, my senses sharp like a razor blade. I toyed with a dirty butter knife on the counter in front of me, thumbing the blunt and toothy blade with the hunger of a wild animal ready to eat. I stared down the clock and watched each second, counting down to ten o'clock.

Ten seconds away from my goal, I could see Dan and the others getting up to leave. He motioned for me, but I shook my head. He insisted, until he realized why I was waiting there. With a smutty smile and a power pump of his hand in the air, he led the group out without a fuss. With them gone, I turned with desperate urgency back to the plastic neon-lit clock on the wall, just as the minute hand took a swing to the right. Ten on the dot.

I sighed, licking my lips in anticipation of all the tastes and scents that were in store for me. If I could just get her to come with me.

The last stragglers left the diner, and it was just me. The silence was killing me and the vibe I was trying to get into right then. My body was preparing. My mind was already there, inching ever closer to what I wanted to do to that girl. What I was *going* to do to her.

I heard her honey-warm voice in the back, talking and giggling. Flirting maybe, I couldn't tell. Her voice was muffled, and I only caught snippets of what she was saying. I didn't care if she was flirting or not. I wasn't interested in her like that. And it was the last she would ever do if I had anything to say about it.

So, go ahead, honey. Flirt away. Leave them wanting more. Leave them a taste they can never get again.

The swinging kitchen door flapped open and there she was. All smiles, her hair down now with a bit of a curl in it from the ponytail. It crowned her round face. She had added some makeup in the back, and it made her glow with a starry vibrance. She was sparkly and bright. My stomach sank as low as it could go. I hadn't expected this. This kind of beautiful right in my grasp. Could she—could she be *Her*—the one I had waited for, for oh so long?

I gulped hard, unable to say anything to her. I

managed a smile, which she returned. She knew how good she looked. She had worked for it, and she knew it was paying off. I realized I had underestimated her and her willingness to do what I wanted. Her creamy, freckled face scrunched up into a funny look.

"I'm not really in the mood for coffee. What do you say we get out of here?"

Damn, she said all the right things.

As we walked out of the diner, the lights inside clicked off and all we had was the flickering light of the streetlamp to light the way. In that yellow strobing light, I caught a glimpse of Dan and one of the girls from work making out by his car. In the middle of the hot and heavy, Dan glanced up and gave me a wink. I nodded his way and smiled. Then my eyes were all for this girl. This possible *One*.

I was trembling all over, bouncing out of my skin just to touch her. She let me hold her hand and I was over the moon. If anyone saw us together that night, it was like a scene from a wholesome romantic movie. The two lovers heading off into the glowing light of the night, hand in hand.

***

Yeah, she was dead. Like dead dead. Like already rotting and definitely not coming back dead. I had fished her out of the murky water of the tub, full of her own filth, and placed her on the tile floor of the bathroom. I kicked her bloated body with my sneaker, and it jiggled and shook, a foul odor emanating from her gaping mouth. I nearly gagged. This was way more than I had bargained for. I had wanted her dead, sure. I had planned it out in my head a hundred times. Fantasized about every step, every moment of it. But I hadn't actually imagined what would happen if my fantasy became this kind of reality. And the truth was, I hadn't killed her.

This had definitely been a case of wrong place, wrong time, and very unlucky me. Instead of heading to my place, she begged and pleaded for us to go to her apartment. It was a warm and inviting place, nothing like the hole in the wall I lived in. She made me comfortable on the couch, and then came the drugs. She had enough to tranquilize a horse buried in her dresser. She offered me some. Of course, I couldn't say no. It would have been impolite.

But a little became a lot as the night burned on into very early morning. I was wasted and she was beyond wasted.

I remember her leaning in close to me and whispering, "You look familiar. Have we met before?"

"Not before tonight, sweetheart," I tried to sound suave, but it just came off like a cheesy line from a bad movie. A movie I was stuck in, clawing to get out, but the room was spinning, and I was spinning with it.

She put her finger to my mouth and shushed me. Her touch lingered on my lips for a long moment as her gaze pounded into mine so sharply, I felt like I could see her thoughts. But that was just the drugs talking.

"I remember you," she said. "You don't remember me."

Her words disturbed me, even in my high, but it was the look in her eye that really scared me. She was serious. I pulled away from her touch and tried to laugh it off, my head rolling backward onto the couch.

"Sure," I said. "I'm not gonna remember anything in the morning anyway. You can count on that."

She tried to kiss me. It tasted like alcohol and nicotine, but the kiss was good. I pushed into her body for more, but she reared back. She stared at me, like really stared at me, as if she could see through my insides to my very soul. I'd never seen a gaze that deep before. Definitely not one bent on me. She opened her mouth to say something, but the words never came.

After a minute, she stumbled to her feet and said she was going to take a bath. That's the last thing I remember.

The next thing I knew, the sun was beaming in my face. From the open window, cold winter air blasted my face. I shivered uncontrollably, my teeth chattering. I blinked in the bright light and tried to get my bearings. Things started to look familiar and then I remembered the girl.

I could hear the water running in the bathroom to my left. The sound of water sloshing and splashing. Reluctantly, I stood up, swaying a bit on my feet. I inched my way toward the bathroom door. It was open just an inch and I couldn't see inside. The water just kept running, the hollow sound of something thumping around in the water making my stomach turn.

Slowly, I opened the door. I was immediately met with water at my feet, that spilled out onto the living room carpet. My sneakers were already squishing around in the inch of water on the floor when I stepped inside the bathroom. In the dim light, I could see her blue-tinged body bobbing in the overflowing tub water and hitting the sides of the tub with a sickening thump.

Her eyes were *wide* open. A look of agony on her creamy, freckled face. I felt like her eyes were watching me and I stumbled back. It was a face with a look of death I had seen before. My mother, my mother in the tub—dead. Her wrists slit and her body swimming in her own pool of blood.

I fell out of the room onto the squishy damp carpet of the living room. I couldn't breathe. Couldn't think. My stomach was sick. Oh, my stomach was sick. My body was trembling like crazy.

The girl. My mother. The girl.

I had to get out of there. I sat up straight, realizing the danger I was in right then. Scrambling to my feet, I headed straight for the door, but I stopped. I retraced my steps, making sure that there was no trace of me left. No sign I had ever been there. Then I hightailed it out of there, slamming the door behind me. I wanted as much distance between me and my mother--I mean the dead girl—as possible.

9 A STOPPING POINT...MAYBE

My mother. My mother was everywhere. Everywhere I looked. Everywhere I went. Everywhere inside me. I couldn't run from her. Couldn't break away. Not after that girl in the tub. That stupid, stupid girl.

I tried everything to get her out. Booze—but that didn't work. Sleep—but she was molded into every dream. Then I tried staying awake—but the thoughts inside my head were hers or of her.

I never wanted to hear that warm, sickly-sweet voice again. How it lulled and cooed at me while she injected her poison into my veins, infecting every part of me until all I became was rotten. Just rotten to the core.

Johnny, be good.

I screamed, shattering my silence like broken glass. How? How could I be good when all she fed me was death? The death of *Me*. With her inside my head, I was nothing but a shell, and that's how she had always liked it. I was compliant then. Johnny was good when Johnny didn't make a sound and did what he was told.

Johnny, be good.

Johnny, be good.

JOHNNY, BE GOOD!

Johnny was good. Johnny was real good—good at what he does. Good at lying. Good at killing. Good at never getting caught. *I would never get caught.*

"Johnny is good, Mama," I whispered in the dark, lying on my bed staring into the night. "Johnny is always good."

I felt the darkness shifting, a familiar shape creeping there in the shadows. I could feel her staring into the deep. Staring straight at me. In my mind's eye, I saw her; that faded blue dress, her wrists slit and blood slowly dripping.

Drip. Drip! DRIP!

The sound of her blood hitting the floor lulled me into a restless sleep. And I dreamed. Dreamed of bathtubs full of blood and my mother's voice calling me in the shadows.

***

I stopped—stopped the blood and the killing. I didn't want to see the blood and remember. Remember *Her*, my mother, with every one of them. So, I tried to be—good. Just like Mama wanted.

The winter crawled by so slowly that I thought I would die in its ice-cold, deathlike grip. The days, hours, minutes, seconds seemed to take a breath and pause before they pushed forward. I was stuck in my own pause, my own breathless waiting room of nothing. Nothing happened. I went to work at a factory. Stood on the assembly line like a zombie, but boy, I did my job. It was easy. Shit comes down the line. You screw the cap, check for dents and breaks, and then send it down the line. Easy. So simple a monkey could do it. I was a well-trained, brainless monkey. Ready to use right out of the box. Batteries included.

Life was boring again, and I hated it here in the city. Too many people. Too many girls. Too many temptations. I was itching to get away, but something, some small voice in me told me to stay. So, I did. You should never listen to the voices in your head. But mine were too much a part of me not to listen. And most of the time, they were right. Except my mother's.

She was like a bug buzzing around my ear, begging and pleading for me to listen. But I didn't listen to her in my head. If I did, I felt like I would tumble and fall into her deep, dark abyss. Tumble down and down and down. And I would never come out, just like she wanted.

As I said, life was boring. It was predictable. I guess that's what I needed right then. I even started therapy on a whim. It was a joke, but at least it was a human being to talk to every week. On Tuesday evenings, I would make the trip downtown to the community center, where this therapist held his sessions for half price. Of course, at half the price, I was probably only getting half of his attention and half of his good advice. You get what you pay for, I suppose.

Every Tuesday, I went, and every Tuesday, we did the same dance around each other. He would ask the same dumb questions and I would give the same dumb answers. Monosyllabic at best. I think he often wondered why the hell I came, week after week. Just my luck, the guy was both patient and persistent. He started getting creative with those same dumb questions, stumping me, and making me think. And I didn't like that. Of course, that was why I was there, I guess, but still...

Today's visit was just as painful.

"Your father left when you were three?"

A nod from me.

"And your mother raised you?"

Another nod as I flicked cigarette ash into his expensive, decorative ash tray. That's all he was going to get today.

"And what was your relationship with your mother like, John?"

Pause. Deep breath. I stared at him long and hard. I wasn't expecting that question. He'd never asked that before. Why would he ask that now?

"John?"

I flinched. My cigarette singed my fingers. I put it out in the ash tray and leaned back in the uncomfortable plastic chair positioned opposite him. I stared him down. He looked awfully smug behind his wire-rimmed glasses, like a spider that's cunning trail of web has finally caught that pesky fly it's been after. Well, I might have been stunned a little, but I wasn't caught. At least, not yet.

"John?"

I woke from my deep, dark thoughts long enough to be angry. I hated when he called me that. That wasn't me. John was my father, a man I never wanted to be like. I simmered in that thought for a long while. He waited, just as patiently as ever. That snotty, sort of stuck up, placid smile plastered on his face. He was older, probably in his fifties, a little gray around the temples and balding in the back. To overcompensate, he had grown himself a rather impressive beard, all salt and pepper, trimmed precisely with a neat mustache. His ugly sweater vests made him even more stuffy. Like in case you didn't know he was rich and well off, his wardrobe sure was a reminder.

I realized I better say something, so I said, "What?" Brilliant, right?

He just smiled politely and calmly said again, "What was your relationship with your mother like?"

I swallowed hard, avoiding his eyes. My foot bobbed up and down with furious speed. I gripped the arms of the plastic chair tightly. And I said nothing. He motioned for me to speak. Pushing, always pushing. I gritted my teeth to keep from screaming in his face.

Finally, I pried open my mouth and said, "Just like any other kid, I guess."

I fished in my pocket for another cigarette. There was one left, bent and nearly broken, but it would have to do. I crammed it into my face and tried to light it.

I heard him say, "Normal?"

Come on, light. Damn it, light!

But it wouldn't. Angrily, I said, "Yeah. What else is there to say?"

Again and again, I tried to light the cigarette. Nothing.

"Can we talk about your relationship with her?" he asked. His voice was like sandpaper on glass.

I shook my lighter, my hands trembling and tried one more time with the cigarette. This time, it lit. I breathed in the precious fumes and let out a sigh of stunted relief with the smoke that followed.

It eased my nerves just enough to say, "Sure."

The therapist nodded, satisfied that he had won that one. Little did he know, I didn't plan on giving an inch.

He started with, "Describe her to me."

"You want me to describe my mother to you?"

"Yes. In detail as you remember her."

Silence, awkward and uncomfortable. I blew smoke his way just to spite him before I started talking. My words came slow at first, rising like a tidal wave ready to push forward in an explosion of deadly force.

"My mother—my mother—my mother. She had short dark hair, kind of a...you know a...pixie cut I think they call it. Real short. She had...uh...brown eyes and cherry-red lips. Always cherry-red. I guess it was lipstick. I was little, so I didn't think about it much. She had a favorite blue dress she always used to wear. It was faded, the flower print on it was so faint it was almost gone, but it made her eyes sparkle. You know the color of the dress, I mean. I didn't like to look at her eyes, the way they sparkled like that. Didn't like them looking at me."

"Why, John?"

"Well, because they scared me. They were like cat eyes—devil eyes. They saw everything. Everything inside you and they knew too much."

I took a long draw from my bent cigarette. I couldn't keep my free hand still, so I gripped the side of the chair clinging on for dear life.

"What frightened you about your mother, John?"

"Who said I was afraid of my mother?" I sat up straight in my chair, ready to leap out of it. Ready to fight.

"You did—"

"I said her eyes scared me." I interrupted him, pointing a finger at him. "Don't you put words in my mouth!"

Losing your cool, Johnny. You're losing it.

The therapist nodded, still very calm, and he said quietly, "Go on, then, John. Tell me what you want and how you want. Alright?"

I nodded, breathing heavily. My mind felt like it was shattering into a million pieces. My heart was beating so fast, I could feel a deep pressure and pain in my chest. And all I saw was *Her*. All I saw was my mother.

I screamed.

***

"Yo, Johnny!"

Dan's voice cut through my clouded thoughts like shards of ice splitting, the water bursting into jagged waves. I remembered to turn and smile. The smile was a little weak, but it would have to do. We were just outside of the factory coming off our night shift. It had snowed a little and a glistening blanket of crisp, fresh snow had settled on all the cars. I hated it.

Dan jogged up to me, his hands crammed into his thick winter coat. He was shivering like crazy, his teeth chattering loudly. He smiled mildly at me.

Amidst his teeth chattering, he managed to say, "H-how are y-you d-doing, man? H-haven't seen you in a w-while. C-can you b-believe this weather? It's f-

79

freezing!"

"Yeah, it's pretty damn cold," I said in my lackluster tone I used those days.

It wasn't cold. Not to me, anyway.

Dear god, do I have to fake that too? This normalcy charade is getting old.

He didn't seem to notice my annoyance or my hesitation. Instead, he chattered out, "You want to go out with us tonight? We're heading out now, actually."

The thought of any amount of time spent in the company of that neanderthal was nauseating. I glanced passed him and caught a glimpse of the gang, shivering out in the cold next to Dan's car. They were all laughing and shouting for him to hurry up. He waved back at them before turning to me rather hurriedly.

"So, how 'bout it, Johnny?"

I made him wait there in the cold for an answer. I already knew what I wanted to say long before he had even asked the question, but I wanted to watch him shiver and squirm while I appeared conflicted and indecisive. It was more fun that way. At least for me. I doubted he was having any fun. I liked that.

"Uhh," I stammered, drawing out my indecision. "I don't know, Dan. I don't really have much luck with your group. Kinda feel like a third wheel, you know?"

For some reason not apparent to me, Dan seemed hurt by that. Maybe he had wanted me to be his wingman for the night. From the looks of it, his odds of stealing everybody's thunder and everybody's girl were pretty good.

I squinted in the early morning sunlight, looking anywhere but at him. I had to listen to him beg and plead for me to come with him, how it wouldn't be fun without me. Blah, blah, blah, blah! Finally, I snapped back at him, screaming in his face. Something mean, something just hurtful enough to shut him up. But for the life of me, after I said it, I couldn't remember what

I'd said. Whatever it was, it left him speechless and afraid. I knew he could see the Hyde in my eyes, the darkness and the anger and the glint of something not quite right that hid there, and I was glad. Maybe then, he would leave me alone.

I didn't wait for him to respond or react or stare one moment longer at me with that dumb, stupefied look of blankness. I turned my back on him. On that whole dumb gang of stupid sheep following a wolf. I didn't look back.

This has to stop, I thought. *This just has to stop.*

But I didn't know what needed to stop now. Do I stop the darkness inside and the rage, or do I stop living a lie and let the darkness take over?

10 THE MUSINGS OF A MUDDLED BRAIN

This is the end—the end of me, the end of everything if I don't figure this out—but what if there isn't more of me than this—what if the only me there is—is a monster—a villain—a devil—a dark thing lurking in the corner that only comes out at night to wreck and ruin and kill—god I love killing—but it isn't really the killing I love it's the aftermath—the bloody mess that's left behind—oh what am I saying—I do love the killing the absolute decimation of a living thing—blood vessels— bursting, skin ripped and torn and all that deliciousness inside that oozes and runs and pours until there's nothing left but flesh and bone—beautiful flesh and bone that I can touch and feel and cherish even if it's just for a moment—that moment is everything—but what comes after is a mess—the question of what to do with the mess I've made—the body that was my momentary playground—what if someone saw or heard something, what if they saw me—oh god what am I doing I could get caught—I am screwed—I am so screwed if I can't get this under control—what if—what if—what if this is all there is of me—what if this is the real me and I can't stop it from rising to the surface and taking control—Hyde can't be stopped I know it—I know it now—there is no way to stop it—it's a rollercoaster ride that won't let me off and I don't want to get off—I don't want to leave until I see every last second of every last kill that I have or will ever make—I want see blood run like a river—flesh and bone cut away like butter—I want to see these women down on their knees and begging for my mercy—begging and crying like prey in the wild—I am the predator—I am the killer—I am the monster in the dark and there is nothing that can stop me now—or ever.

11 MY LIFE AS A HUMAN AUTOMATON

I opened my apartment door that night to find two detectives glaring me up one side and down the other. I was plastered enough to be calm and taciturn, not a shiver or a shake from me. I smiled at them, keeping the door open just a few inches so that they could see just enough of me.

"Is there something the matter, officers?" I said without a stammer.

Good, Johnny. Good.

One of the officers smiled back, a little forced, but I expected as much from a cop. "Mr. John—" he started.

"Johnny. My name's Johnny. John was my father," I finished it for him.

The cop smiled again with a nod of his head. "Can we come in?"

Shit, shit, shit.

There wasn't enough booze in my system not to panic now. I *was* smart enough to keep my eyes from growing wide and scared.

Just be cool, Johnny. There's nothing to hide.

There was everything to hide. And I wasn't even sure yet what they were after, but if they wanted inside my home, it couldn't be good.

"No problem," was all that I could muster.

I spread a plastic smile on my face and kept it there as I opened the door wide to let them in. I stepped aside as they entered, then followed them into my living room/kitchen/bedroom.

"Not much to see," I said with a little chuckle.

They weren't amused.

Oh, God. Was this about the girl in the tub? Was this about #8? #7? #6? #5? Shit, why were there so many of them? What the hell was wrong with me? I should've stopped at one.

I could still taste the sweetness of #1, cherry-red and a bloody beautiful mess. Oh god, could they see what I was thinking? Could they see the wild excitement in my eyes as I thought about her? About all of them?

Don't be stupid, Johnny.

Don't be stupid. Right. Just be cool. Play it cool. Right.

They were looking around, helping themselves to a tour of my tiny living space. I cocked my head to the side as I watched them. I was curious what brought them here. I was even more curious that they would come all this way just to look at my beer can collection and my tower of Chinese takeout boxes. What did these mundane and rather stupid things of mine tell them?

They didn't say a word. They just kept looking.

Finally, I got the gumption to at least keep their ears company while their eyes feasted on what was left of my egg roll and shrimp lo mein sandwich. Yum.

"You want some? It's my own invention," I chimed in.

The one cop turned to me, looking confused. I pointed.

"The sandwich. It's my own invention. Saves time with Chinese leftovers. Makes it easier to carry around while you're doing stuff. Or lounging in the bed. Don't make a mess that way."

Not too much gabbing. Not too much now. Play the part. Be—normal.

Normal? What the hell did I know about that? Well, I'd have to figure it out real quick. They weren't impressed with my sandwich making skills. They weren't much impressed with me either. I had to turn this around.

"Can I get you a glass of water? I don't have bottled, and the tap water runs a little warm, but—"

The cop cut me off before I had finished. "We're fine. Thank you."

I didn't reply. Just kept quiet and stood there awkwardly as they turned to me. One of them motioned for me to sit down. There wasn't anything but the small futon, so I let them sit down there while I sat on the side of my bed. I sat up straight, my hands laying in my lap, like a good little altar boy. I was good, alright. They had to see that.

They stared at me for the longest minute of my life. The smiling cop wasn't smiling anymore. In fact, he looked very, very serious. He eyed me sharply, though I could tell that he was trying hard to appear relatable. Calm, cool, and collected, just your friendly neighborhood police officer. Nothing threatening at all here.

He hemmed and hawed a little, showing his rookie side, before he finally got out, "So, John, you work at the local factory, correct?"

"Well, yeah, I do," I said a little hesitantly. "Been working there for a while now."

"Were you acquainted with Miss Helena Briggs, who also previously worked there?"

"Who?"

"Helena Briggs."

Ugh. That ugly fat girl with the floral nightmare of an apartment. Damn it.

"I'd seen her around, yeah," I said. "We weren't friends or anything."

"Did you ever see her outside of work?"

"What?" I cleared my throat to hide the caution in my voice.

"Did you see Helena Briggs outside of work?"

"You mean, romantically?" I slowed my words down to seem calm and collected, though I was anything but that.

"Or amicably?" the cop shrugged.

No big deal. Just connecting the dots to this grisly murder.

Damn it.

"Did you maybe go out with her and some friends from work? Did you happen to meet her at a bar or a restaurant? Anything like that?"

My mind was racing a thousand miles a minute and my mask of calm was starting to chip away. Was it getting hot in here? No, cold. Definitely hot. I could feel the sweat beading on my clammy forehead. They could see it. I know they could see it.

Choose your words wisely, Johnny boy.

"Sure, we met up with some friends from work a couple times. Even went on a date with her once. Wasn't anything special if you know what I mean?" I chuckled.

They didn't and I cleared my throat again to fill the awkward silence.

Mr. Smiles-A-Lot wasn't happy anymore or even pretending to be friendly. He leaned forward, his hands clasped together in his lap, like he was praying. "Were you aware that she had been killed last summer?"

The way he looked at me, it felt like he already knew the answer.

"Yeah, sure," I said as apathetic and unemotional as possible. More sweat trickled down to my ears, my knee was bobbing up and down. Thud-thud-thud-thud-thud! The cop noticed and I quickly stopped it, gulping hard.

But something grew in me. Something bold in me. I realized they must have asked every other guy from work that she'd ever been with the same questions. For all I knew, I wasn't even on their radar. Just a blip in the system while they sorted out the details of her life to try and solve the crime. If I was lucky, they never would.

Luck has nothing to do with it. You're smart. You're a master at your craft.

If I was so damn smart, why was I making such stupid, stupid mistakes. First, this girl and then the girl in the tub.

I shivered just to think of that one. If I had known her name, I would have burned it from my memory. But for me, she had no name, none of them did. I didn't want them to. Still, she wasn't gone. Her lifeless, bloated body banging against the sides of her tub were engrained in my mind forever.

"John?"

The cops were looking at me strangely. I realized they had asked me another question, but I hadn't heard it. I whipped up some sorry look of concern, a little tremble of the lip and a twinge in my eye, as if a tear could come trickling down at any second.

"Terrible. Just terrible. I-I didn't know her well, but I knew her enough to know she was a nice girl. What happened to her was just terrible."

I hung my head low for dramatic effect. It also gave me the freedom to unload my empathetic mask, loosen the facial muscles into something much more natural for me.

Clever boy.

"So did you know her?"

My head shot up, fast and furious. I tried to put the likeable face back on, but it wouldn't stick. I was left with an empty canvas on which nothing could be written. The not-so-smiley cop cocked his head to the side, looking at me closely—curiously.

I stumbled and stuttered on this one. "I-I, uh—yeah, I knew her. A little. Like I said."

"Do you remember about when you and Miss Briggs went out on a date, like you said?"

When did we go out on the godawful date? I tried peeling back the folds of my memory. The weeks and days since that terrible night. But whatever kind of sick I was that night had messed up and scrambled what memories I had of her. I was left with a garbled mess of minutes and seconds that barely strung together the event. I knew I had killed her. That was about it. Of course, I couldn't tell them that and I wasn't stupid enough to.

So, I told the honest truth, "I don't remember."

"Was it in the spring, maybe? Or maybe in the summer? Do you remember any details?"

Yeah, it was burning hot. And then there was the earthy smell of marijuana creeping through the walls from the neighbors. And that awful warm champagne. I could almost vomit just at the thought of it. Must have been summer.

"Spring, maybe," I said, faking my uncertainty.

The cop nodded with a sigh. He was getting nowhere with me. He paused for a long minute. I bet he was trying to figure out if one more question would do any good. He gave it a shot, but he guessed wrong.

"Do you remember what she was wearing the last time you saw her?"

Good question. Smart. To see if it would jog my memory about our date, the last time I saw her. To see if there was some little dot of connection between me and that dumb girl.

And here I was, the human automaton. Flip my switch and I light up with all the right faces and all the right answers. I'll even shed a tear on command. Well, the switch had been flipped and I sat up straight with a meaningful and sad look on my face. I thought about his question for a moment, or at least, I pretended to think about it. In my head, I could still see her hot pink blazer and white blouse with red hearts on it. Her dress pants were red too. Fire engine red. White socks and white flats. A million jingling bracelets on her chubby arms. Dangly heart-shaped earrings. Her hair was up in a ponytail with a hot pink scrunchie. Ugh, yeah, I remembered. But I said—

"Ugh, lemme see. Well, I think the last time I saw her *was* on that date. I mean, talked to her and such. I think—I, uh, don't have the best memory about these kinds of things, but I think she was wearing a floral dress…uh… it was pink. I think, but other than that, I don't really remember. Guys, right? We don't pay attention to the little details."

I chuckled a little. This time, they laughed too. And with that, the cop who had been speaking, slapped his hands down on his legs and gave me a nod. An unsatisfied and rather frustrated nod, but all the same, it was a nod. Then he stood up, the other cop followed suit, and they headed toward the door.

"Thank you, John," the cop said. "Thank you for your help. You take care now, alright?"

He took one last glance around as he walked to the door. He stopped just short of it, glancing at something on a bookshelf. I didn't know what he saw, but before I could make my way over there to look, he smiled at me and walked away from it. At the door, he didn't stop. He closed it softly behind him and his partner.

I sat in the middle of my apartment, breathing heavily. Sweat still pouring down my face, collecting in between my armpits and my thighs. I waited. Waited for them to come back. To think of something else they wanted to ask or something else they wanted so desperately to see. Maybe they wanted to dig through my trash or take me downtown to question me more. But they didn't come back. There was no more knocking at the door, just the heavy silence.

After a long moment, I finally breathed a sigh of relief. Until I remembered what the officer had been looking at so curiously on my bookshelf. The only one that I had. Warily, I leaned my head to the side to see it better, but that wasn't helpful. I edged closer to the bookshelf. Slowly. Slowly. Until I saw it. My little box of treasures. The things I kept from all my adventures. All my kills. It was partially open. Open just a crack. Enough for a bit of hot pink scrunchie to poke out of the side.

Damn it, Johnny.

12 MY LITTLE BOX OF TREASURES (AKA THE KILL BOX)

AN ITEMIZED LIST OF THE CONTENTS OF MY KILL BOX:

1) 1 PAIR OF RED LACE PANTIES

2) 1 DRIVE-IN THEATER TICKET

3) 1 WINE BOTTLE CORK

4) 1 BLOODY, BENT CIGARETTE

5) 1 HOT PINK SCRUNCHIE (PIECES OF HAIR ATTACHED)

6) 1 KARAMBIT KNIFE (CLEANED)

7) 1 BEST FRIENDS BEADED BRACELET WITH THE NAME "BOBBIE JO"

8) 1 WELL WORN RUBBER BAND FROM OFF HER WRIST (SHE MUST HAVE HAD A LOT OF MENTAL ISSUES)

9) ...NOTHING...I GOT NOTHING

13 A TROPHY FOR #9 AND HER

My kill box lay open on the coffee table, its contents carefully spilled out on the bed next to me. I lay with them, drunk with the memory of each one. Relishing them. Reveling in them. I could feel myself pulling back from the present, peeling back the tissue and membrane that clouded the past, until I could see them all so clearly. Mmm, what an intoxicating trip down memory lane.

I shouldn't have opened the box. I should have closed it tight after the visit from the cops. Closed it tight and hidden it away. Or better yet, I should have destroyed it. Gotten rid of it for good. But I was attached to that little box and to the precious things inside. My trophies for being a good boy—a very good boy.

As I lay on the bed in the semi-darkness of early evening, I played with the hot pink scrunchie. I smelled it, breathed it in deeply. I didn't like it. It smelled like hairspray and her perfume. God, she must have dipped her entire body, hair and all, in that disgustingly sweet fragrance. It was awful. But I couldn't stop smelling it, taking in the sickly-sweet smell of the kill. Of power and success. I smiled, letting the scrunchie fall to my chest. It bobbed up and down with every breath, amusing me as I closed my eyes and daydreamed.

This was the best part of all this, even better than the killing. Laying curled up among my spoils like a dragon in his keep. Sleeping with one eye open and ready to protect what was mine. I could relive every blessed moment of each one, in the safety of my lair. No other eyes on me, nosing around and judging me. I could be me—the real me. Not the version of me that everyone saw, that I let them see. But the *real me*. The monster buried just under the surface.

Not so fast, Johnny. What did they see?

My eyes shot open, my halcyon bubble burst as I remembered like a shot in the dark. The cop had seen my kill box. Damn it, he had seen it, its contents spilling out like a kid vomiting on a thrill ride. It just screamed, "Look! Look at me!"

My quiet and my comfort were slashed and spoiled. I tossed the scrunchie back in the box and quickly gathered up the rest of the treasures, stuffing them inside. I slammed the box lid down. Shut it and locked it good and tight. No one was going to see what was inside, not even me.

My collection was incomplete. I had nothing for #9. A mistake on my part. I had been too high and too scared out of my wits to remember to take anything. I was kicking myself now. Holding the box in both hands, I could feel the emptiness inside where #9's treasure should be. The others inside, they felt it too. They wanted to be whole too. Complete. Perfect.

That's when I decided on ten. #10 was going to be the biggest, the best, and the last. I wanted to put this craving to bed, but I wanted to go out with a freaking *bang*. And #10 seemed like the perfect one to do it.

There was still the matter of #9. Even if I got #10, the collection still wouldn't be complete. I had to fix it. I had to fix #9. I decided to fix it that night. I remembered where she lived. There was still a chance that her belongings hadn't totally been cleared away. I had to try to get something to remember her by. Anything would do at this point.

So, on that icy cold night, I tumbled out of my apartment with nothing on but my white undershirt, worn-out jeans and sneakers. The sky was threatening snow, spitting little frozen pellets of ice on my bare head and naked arms. A storm was on its way. A big one. But I didn't care. I didn't even notice. I was hyper-focused on the task at hand. My little adventure for buried treasure.

I walked for what seemed like forever in that cold, before an old man driving slowly by pulled to the side and offered a ride. He was bald, his features buried in wrinkles and whiskers. He didn't much like to talk and I liked the calm silence as we drove. He asked me where I was going and that was it. Said he'd get me there in no time. Long before the storm would hit.

Sitting there in the warm pick-up truck gave me time to think. What the hell was I doing? A blizzard was on its way and here I was gallivanting in the dark for a prize. Call it obsessive. Call it crazy. But I had to have it. Something in that girl's apartment, something of hers, was begging to be mine. There was nothing for it. I had to oblige.

I watched the few first flakes of snow begin to fall outside the passenger side window, skating and flurrying passed with electric speed. This was going to be a bad one.

"You got a home, son? A place to stay?" the man chimed in, his voice soft like velvet and suede.

It made me feel safe and comfortable, lulling me almost to sleep. I realized it was late and I must look pretty crazy wandering the streets in the dark before a storm.

Quietly, I said, "Yeah, but I didn't want to be there."

He nodded, stewing over my words for a long time.

"I get that. The road always looks better than the place we're meant to be. It calls you. I get that."

He was a deep thinker. I could almost watch the wheels turning inside his head while he drove through the snow. It was getting heavy. I turned back to the window.

"But you make sure you don't stay away from home too long. There's a pull there that we can't ignore, no matter how much we want to. It makes up what we are and heals us when we're broken. Home is good. And it's where we're meant to be. Sometimes we just have dress it up a bit, you know?"

He looked at me like no one has ever looked at me before. It made me both intrigued and sorely uncomfortable. It was a look of genuine friendship and kindness. That was something that I had never known, never really understood until now. It made me not want to leave the warmth and the safety of this truck with its earthy smell of tobacco and its tacky Christmas tree freshener that smelled like lemon scented fabric softener. It made me want to hold on to this strange feeling of contentment and belonging. Until he said—

"You got a girl?"

I gritted my teeth and kept quiet. The magic moment was over, and I was wondering how hard it would be to get him to pull over. Snow or no snow, I wasn't here for a lecture from a nosy old man. Needless to say, I didn't answer.

He seemed to feel the awkwardness of the moment, the tension rising in the air, because he cleared his throat—more of a hacking gag given the amount of chewing tobacco and cigarette remnants I saw at my feet.

"Now, I know that's none of my business. But I bet you do got a girl. And I bet she's waiting for you at home."

The car stopped. We were here. He turned to me with that warm and sincere look of an honest to goodness friend and he gently prodded, "You go on and get home now, you hear? It's a hell of a night to go wandering in dark places. Even in here." And he tapped my head lightly with his gnarled, dirty old finger.

He gave me a toothy smile—well some of his teeth were missing and all the ones he had left were stained a sickening yellow—and waited for me to get out.

I didn't smile back, but I did say, "Thanks."

Then I slid out of the truck and slammed the door behind me. I didn't look back, but I imagine he went along his way and made it to wherever home was for him.

***

There was no yellow tape across the diner girl's apartment door anymore. You could see remnants of it here and there, and places where it had pulled up the crappy white paint around the door frame. I stared at the door for the longest time, the old man's words running senselessly through my brain.

Home, I had a place to live, but not a home. Not like the kind he had been talking about. The kind you were proud to belong to, to come from, to go back to when you were tired of the road and the world in general. This had been her home. Probably her safe haven, her delight at the end of a long, long day. Or maybe, just maybe, she was as miserable as me wherever she was, and this was just another lousy steppingstone to nothing. Because in the end, that's all life is, a big, wide pile of nothing.

With that sentiment in mind, I picked the lock and opened the door. No one saw me. There was no one to see me. The hallway light was out, and it was late. Everyone was hunkered down for the storm that was now in full swing outside. I could hear the wind howling even through the thick walls of the apartment building. It was going to be a long walk home. I didn't have to worry about that just yet. I was here on business.

I tiptoed my way into the apartment. It felt like I was stepping into a holy shrine that was built just for me. Sure, she wasn't my kill or anybody's for that matter. Still, I had claim to her. I felt it in my bones. She was mine. Just like all the others.

The room I was in was dark. Outside the windows, the snow swirled and whirled wildly. The night sky was a dull grey above the cluttered glow of the city lights. I took a moment to admire the violence of the storm before I took another look around me. It was like going into a candy store and everything was free. I could take anything. Anything I wanted to remember her by. To remember that night as something more than the horrible nightmares and heroin.

Out of the corner of my eye, I saw that the door to the bathroom was open. The darkness within eerily taunting me. The carpet in front of the door had been ripped up where the water from the overflowing tub had spilled into the living room. I didn't want to look at the bathroom or its goading open door.

But I did.

I quickly found myself at its threshold, staring with the fear of a little child at the door to a very haunted house.

It's not haunted, Johnny. Just a little tainted. Stained. Spoiled.

Rotten, it was rotten. Just like me. Spoiled by what happened inside. It would never be unspoiled.

Slowly, my hand reached for the door. I took a deep breath and pushed it all the way open. It screeched and whined as it revealed the room within, ghostly white and eerily quiet. The quiet wrapped itself around me like a blanket, stiflingly hot and suffocating. I couldn't breathe.

Take a breath, stupid.

I did what I was told. After all, I was a good boy. My eyes immediately darted to the bathtub. It was empty now. Devoid of water and a body. Still, I could hear that persistent banging sound, like the body was still beating against the sides of it. I cringed at the thought, acid rising in my throat.

No, I wouldn't throw up. Not here. Not in her bathroom. Not next to that tub, staring it down while I expelled my guts. I swallowed it down with difficulty, but I did it.

I turned my eyes away from the room. I turned away and tried to leave it behind. As I walked away, I thought I caught a glimpse of a shadow within the shadows, deep and dark and black as pitch. It was watching me. Let it watch. Let it take me in as I pillaged and burned down the memory of her.

I made my way to her room in the darkness. The door was open, inviting me in like a lover to a sweet repose. It wasn't floral. It wasn't much of anything. For a girl as pretty as she had been, it seemed it was all a façade to hide something that was both empty and screaming. She was broken and perhaps I had only broken her more. Two broken people had found each other and drowned each other in their tears.

Her bed was draped in dark gray sheets and a black comforter. Black. I didn't expect that. She seemed so bubbly pink and perfect. The picture of her home painted a picture of a girl much different. A goth princess, a little okay and a lot messed up. Her bed looked so inviting and imagining her in it made me want to feel it more. I found myself sinking deep into those cheap cotton sheets, cool and all too nice. I sighed with perfect contentment. This was nice. It would have been nicer if I wasn't alone. But I couldn't have everything.

The snow outside the window was heavy and wild, the wind screaming and pounding against the sides of the apartment building, like a banshee. But it lulled me into a peaceful, quiet sleep. I felt myself sink deeper and deeper. Somewhere in the darkness of the night, I felt a gentle hand caress my cheek.

***

I woke up and the world was silent and blue. It was cold, so cold I could see my breath as I let out a loud, exaggerated yawn. I curled up tightly into the black down comforter and stared out of the window. The air outside looked crisp and clear, the sun just rising over the horizon in hues of pink and red. The blue-tinged remnants of the night were quickly vanishing, replaced if not with warmth, at least the promise of it. I could see the rooftops of the buildings all around weighted down with snow drifts at least three feet high. They were sloped and curved like white sand dunes. As the light wind scurried across the tops of them, a billowy dust of snow crystals scattered through the air, twinkling, and sparkling in the sunlight.

The world was calm and quiet, and I hated it. Quiet like this made my brain, already chaotic and loud, all the louder. Too loud for me to shut out what I did not want, and only getting louder. I began to squirm within the cocoon I had created for myself, already restless.

Angsty and antsy, I crawled my way out of the warmth of the bed and began to wander the room. It was like tiptoeing my way through a closed museum, tasting the delights of someone else's life without the trouble of making their acquaintance. Like an all-access pass to feel what it's like to be someone else. Not that I wanted to be someone else. I didn't mind being me, most of the time. Sometimes I wondered whether everyone else was just like me, or what made me—*Me*. I wondered if there was something in everyone. That thread of storm clouds and chaos that pushed them to the edge and over, just like me.

She wasn't much for knick-knacks or frivolous ornaments. It looked like she had curated an odd assortment of things that meant something only to her. A busted music box that still played but off-key and too slow, like it came straight from a horror movie prop box. A beaten-up stuffed koala bear that was missing an eye, its stuffing streaming out of its seams in ghostly trails. A hair bow that was tattered and frayed, something that I would have expected a girl like the one I met in the diner to wear. It had a soft, fluffy layer of dust on it where it lay on her vanity. It hadn't seen the light of day in a long time. She must have outgrown it, grown tired of it, or perhaps, it just didn't suit her style anymore. Either way, it was perfect for my collection.

I started to pick it up but stopped. No, this was too easy. I wasn't choosing carefully enough, and anyway, this didn't really show who she was. This was a ghost of who she had been a long time ago. I wanted a piece of the girl I had met.

No, I needed to look further. So, I did. Soon enough, I found a wooden box of trinkets, odds and ends of her past. There were a dozen friendship bracelets, cut in two and faded. Obviously, from the looks of them, the friendship had ended and badly. I dug deeper in the box to find a pair of ticket stubs to a play from six years ago. Probably from a date she wanted to remember well. There was a couple of polaroid pictures ripped in two. I pieced them together to see a much younger her, perhaps in her late teens, sucking the face off of some stupid kid who looked like he must have had about two brain cells to rub together.

"Must have cheated on you. Dirty damn kid," I muttered to the pictures. To her. Not that she could hear me.

I glared that dumb kid down as I put the pieces of the polaroids back into the box. I put the box back. I didn't want any of that. It seemed too sacred. Too untouchable, even for me.

I had almost given up my search when something sparkled in the corner of my eye. It was a silver-plated mirror, an antique. It was covered with a cakey dusting of drugs, but it still caught the light from the window and gleamed. On top of its glass surface, I saw her work name tag. I read her name a dozen times to myself, muttering it over and over again.

"Julianna."

Didn't know her last name. Just that, Julianna. Pretty name for a pretty girl. Saying it out loud, the sound of it shivered up and down my spine, like a magical current of sexual tension that hit the air and fizzled out because she wasn't there. Not anymore.

I hadn't remembered her name. She had probably told it to me, but I didn't pay attention. I never did with any of these girls. I wasn't going to know them long enough to want to remember a name tagged to my body count. Like farm animals, it was best not to name them. Naming them gave them character— Personhood. I didn't want them to be people to me. Just things. Things I could take. Things I could destroy.

But her—*Julianna*. She was different. I wanted to know her. I wanted to remember her. I wanted—

A hot cold shiver ran through my entire body.

Oh, God. She was it. It was her—she was *Her*. The one I had been looking for, the one I had dreamed about, wished for, and desired for so long. I had missed her. Lost her in the moment I had her in my hands. She had slipped through like water and sand in the storm of my own reflection. I had lost the only thing that I had ever wanted.

Yes, she was dead. Yes, I was going to kill her, regardless of whether she was the one or not, and especially if she *was* the one. But now, that idea seemed frivolous, a rotten waste. Just rotten. Why would I kill the one thing that I desired?

Because you're rotten, Johnny. And blood is all there is in that rotten storm inside your head. Blood is everything. Blood and chaos.

I grimaced. Here I was standing amid greatness,

and I hadn't killed her. Didn't even earn the right to a trophy because she wasn't my kill. She wasn't anyone's kill. She had offed herself in a tempest of misery and depression that she had tried to drown out with those drugs. She had died and I had missed it. The beautiful release of a beautiful thing.

I could feel myself become both terrified and angry, my body still shivering and shaking with the realization of my perfect girl. Julianna.

"Julianna," I whispered.

I took the name tag and hurried out of the room. I didn't want to stay anymore. Not when I had spoiled it. Not when she wasn't mine. Not really.

I closed the door to her apartment quietly behind me and tiptoed down the hall. As I hit the frigid morning air, I took a deep and desperate breath to ease the panic and the aching in my chest. The morning seemed both exciting, new, and very, very tragic all at once. I had found *Her* and lost her in the same breath.

And now—what?

14 LIVING IN PARADISE WITH MY WORST NIGHTMARE

*I*n my dream, I met her at a bar, one of several I
visited that night. This one happened to be my
favorite, and despite already being plastered, I settled
into a bar stool, ready for a long night and a good time.
The bar was packed, an oddity for a Tuesday in the
middle of winter, but I picked her out of the crowd in a
split second.

Julianna.

She was taller than I remembered. Her slinky,
braless number seemed out of place on a frigid
February night in a questionable dive bar. It looked like
she was ready for a night club. I cocked my head to the
side to get a better look at her.

Sensing my eyes on her, she stopped mid-step in
the midst of the crowd and cocked her pale face to the
side with a quirky smile. She looked at me like she
knew me. I couldn't help but smile at that.

"Ronny!" she exclaimed above the noise of the
crowd. "Is that you?"

No wonder she looked at me the way she did. She
did think she knew me. I guess I must have looked a lot
like someone else. Someone she liked very much,
because she came running up to me, her glittering dress
shifting and sparkling in the dim neon lights of the bar.
With a squeal of delight, she wrapped her thin arms
around me and squeezed until I couldn't breathe. It was
a long hug, but it didn't feel awkward. It felt like we
were whatever she thought we were, old friends or

lovers meeting by chance. Like our bodies knew one another well. I slipped into her arms like a well-fit glove. It was almost magic until she started talking.

She belched before pulling back to look at me with a drunken giggle. I could smell the booze coming off her.

"Sorry about that," she said, still giggling. "It's been one of those nights. And one of those days. And nights and days. And nights and days. Ha! Try a year of that shit and you can see why I'm here tonight."

She stumbled into a seat next to me, wedging herself between me and a large man in the next seat over whose body spilled out on all sides. She wriggled a little against his side, looking rather perturbed.

"Boy, either these seats are getting smaller," she said loudly, "or my buddy over here needs to suck it in."

The large man didn't pretend not to notice. He glared her down. and me beside her.

"Tell your friend here to watch her mouth." he said to me with a grumbling, gravelly voice.

The girl smirked and guffawed loudly. "Tell him to watch his weight."

What a tongue! This was my kind of girl. I couldn't help but smile. That only got me a wicked look from the fat man. He stood up, and he was much, much taller than I had first guessed. Much, much taller than me. I gulped hard as my head went back and back to take all of him in. I saw him clench his fists until his knuckles turned white. I knew then that this wasn't going end well.

"You think that's funny, kid?" the fat man demanded.

I should have kept my mouth shut. I should have. But I was three sheets to the wind already and any inhibitions or rational thoughts of caution were far behind me at that point. I smirked back, nice and wide.

"Not as funny as you trying to find your ass," I said.

I laughed. Julianna laughed. The fat man didn't. He punched me square in the face. I should have been thrown to the floor by that much force, but this was a dream. I took it like a man and turned a bloody face back to him with as much fierce indignation as I could muster. It must have been the dream. It must have been the magic in the air. It must have been the black-eyed glare I gave him. Whatever it was, he turned tail and headed straight out of the door. He didn't even pay for his drink.

I could hear Julianna laughing hysterically behind me. I joined in, turning to her with a wide smile. Without a word, she took my hand in hers—it was warm and soft and gentle—and she led me out of the bar. Out into the quiet of the winter night.

Both of us took a deep breath in the cold night air, watching our breath rise up in cotton clouds to the stars. It was snowing. Not like the blizzard, but soft and slow, like a myriad of dancers in a ballroom masquerade. And we were invited.

She turned to me with a smile. It was enchanted and beautiful. Her eyes were sparkling in the dim light, the glitter on her face and her dress shining like the sun on a clear winter day. She was the sun. She was—

She looked at my bloodied face with a sorry smirk and raised her hand to my face. I veered away from her touch.

"I'm a mess. Don't want to get you all bloody."

She only smiled, pushing her body closer to mine in the cold and dark. She gently wiped the blood away with her delicate fingers. Her touch was like a shock to my system, incredible and terrifying, all wrapped up in her small, warm hand.

"It brings us together," she whispered with an intoxicating hiss.

And then her lips were on mine. I resisted at first, but the touch of her lips was like fire and sun and light. Life itself to my dead and cold heart. So, I gave in, pressing myself hard into her body. I was hungry for her kiss, and she fed me with the same sweet passion.

I closed my eyes and she pulled away.

Then came the smell. A rotten, sickly-sweet concoction of what could only be death, refuse and spoiled things. It tinged and burned my nostrils with a familiar tang. It rotted in my stomach and left me eating acid. The taste of her upon my lips turned sour. I tried to lick it away, but it stayed like a sticky slime that smelled of sulfur.

I opened my eyes, startled by the sensations and the smells. And there she was. Not Julianna. Not anymore. It was my mother. Her body was rotted and decayed, bloated, and dripping with mold and old blood. Her wrists were slit open, the wounds filled with creeping, crawling maggots. She smiled at me with her wicked two-faced smile, and I vomited.

"It's what brings us together, Johnny," she hissed.

I screamed, blasting the night, the darkness, and her away.

***

I woke up, trembling all over and sweating. I was in my own bed. In my own apartment. Hidden in the dark of another winter night, clinging to Julianna's name tag so tightly that it had made a deep impression in my palm. Suddenly, I was afraid of it. Afraid of her. Of Julianna. Of my mother. Somehow in my mind, in that moment, they melded into one. One painful, dangerous woman that I knew would be the end of me.

I lay there in the night, staring up into the darkness, and waited. I waited for the end. But it didn't come—only the morning.

15 THE DANGERS OF BEING HUNGRY

The whispers had started at work. Eyes on me when they thought I didn't notice. But I wasn't stupid. I heard the talk around the old water cooler. The murder investigation for #5, aka Helena Briggs, was underway and gaining speed. It was all over the news and on the lips of everyone at work. The women there were afraid. Everyone was. And like I said, every eye was on me.

I don't think they suspected me, not really. But I *was* the last one to see her. I found out that Dan had made sure that everyone, including the police, knew that part. If I wasn't already a social pariah before, I certainly was now. That jerk wad kept his distance, for good reason. I spread my own rumors about him around the good old water cooler. Just for fun.

"Hey, have you heard about Dan..."

Pretty soon, he was his own kind of pariah. None of the women would touch him with a ten-foot pole, let alone go out with him. He wasn't seeing any kind of action. I knew that for a fact. So, I spread a little more around. It didn't matter if it was true. The women, and even the men, believed it as honest to goodness truth. That's because everybody really hated Dan. After a while, the talk around the factory was just about good old Dan and not about me.

It was fun spreading poison to the sheep who were stupid enough to listen. For as you must know, people in general are as brilliant as a flock of sheep. They spook easily and they believe just about anything you tell them if you use the right words, the right inflection, and the right facial expressions. If you look just as afraid as you figure they will be, the fear in them just comes easily. Like flood waters that breach a levy. *Boom!* Levy breaks, and they're putty in your hands. You can mold them any way you want, push their beliefs, and their terror, in any direction you please. They are yours. Dear Dan was already pounded down to playdough between my fingers, and about to break. I was enjoying myself immensely. *And* it kept me from thinking about my own problems, the poison in my own veins that was Her.

I got a little mischievous as winter took a strong hold over the city. I decided to spread a little holiday cheer and made my way to a payphone to make an anonymous call to the police. I told them all about Dan. Everything and anything, real or invented that would turn their heads toward him. When I was done, I had painted a very pretty picture of a man who might just be a killer. I was very proud of my dramatic performance as the concerned citizen, just out there trying to keep the women of this city safe from guys like Dan—or really, guys like me.

I didn't see Dan for a while after that. He seemed to have been wiped off the face of the earth. A few days before Christmas, as I was heading into the factory for my shift, good old Dan caught up with me. He was windblown and flushed, looking all hot and bothered.

"Hey!" he yelled after me, but I didn't deign to stop. So, he ran for me. "Hey, you son of a bitch! You, look at me!"

He yanked me around to face him. He was a good bit taller than I was, and he loomed over me with such a glare of pure hate that I almost laughed with delight. I had done that. I had whittled him down to a monstrous mess, all for the price of a girl.

He leaned in close to me, a solitary stubby finger

poking at my chest while he talked his big stuff.

"I don't know what kind of game you think you're playing. But if you ever spread shit about me again, I'll knock your brains out of your head so fast, you won't even know you're dead until your body hits the ground. You understand?"

I said nothing, reveling in this moment of weak confrontation. He was all talk, I knew that. Big talk for a big man, with a little brain and little sense. I turned away from him without a word. He was quick to whip me back around. His eyes were feverishly wild, a hint of tears lining their red rims.

"You don't understand what you've done. They're looking at me."

"Who?" I said, cool and calm. "Who's looking at you, Dan?"

He mussed his hair with both his shaking hands and sighed with a weight that held the world.

"Everyone," he whispered loudly. "You don't know what you've done, Johnny. They're all looking at me like some kind of freak. The cops are even thinking twice about me—you know, 'coz of all those missing girls. They've gotten wind of my name. Stopped by my house a few times. Just checking, they said. Asking me questions. I know they're watching me, and I know it's coz of you. I know it. So, you can't say anything else about me. Not to anyone, you hear? I—I can't take anymore, alright?"

Now, a decent person would have stopped the ruse right there, seeing this man falling apart. A good man would have helped another man out of this predicament, taken him under his wing and cleared his name. But I was neither decent nor good, and I was enjoying every damn second of this.

Bring the popcorn! The show has only just started, my friend.

So, I put on my best smile, cocky and full of as much shit as I could muster. Chest puffed out and head held high to reach even close to his height. And then—

"Get used to the madness," I whispered. "This is your new reality, my friend."

"I don't want this!" He was frantic now.

My smile only got wider. "Of course, you do, Dan. You wanted all eyes on you. You wanted all the ladies to know your name. Now they do. Everyone knows who Dan the Man is. A womanizer and maybe worse. Believe me, the truth will come out, sooner rather than later."

He was breathless and lost for words. So, I finished it for him, "Welcome to hell."

With those three words left to rattle about in his brain, I turned away from him. He didn't follow this time. He just stood there looking dumbstruck and scared. All eyes were on him, while I slipped into the crowd and disappeared. Something I was very good at doing.

***

In the dark of night, as I lay alone in my bed surrounded by the deadly quiet, the poisonous grip of *Her* crept up on me and consumed me. Two shadows were slowly becoming one and watching me from the deepest darkness. Julianna and my mother. Before long, it was impossible to decipher where one ended and the other began. In my mind, they had become the same, meshing into something both beautiful and rotten. Something that soured my stomach and turned my insides into rot. A monster—and I was afraid of it. I was afraid of the dark.

Julianna's name tag had ceremoniously joined the other things in the box. I expected them to welcome her with open arms and loud applause. After all, she was the *One*. But it was silent as I placed the little metal tag into the velvet lined box next to the hot pink scrunchie. #5 did not even welcome #9. Instead, from the box I heard weeping. Women weeping. All of them were in tears, I could hear it. Feel it.

She's not the last. Not the last. Only one of us. There will be others. Many, many others.

A shiver ran through me. I could feel them all rushing toward me, screaming. Screaming at the top of their lungs if they had any. I could feel the force of them, the coldness of their touch, but I wasn't afraid. Not of them. They were mine. My little collection of ladies. Dan could get them for a night, but mine, I had forever and ever. I was the king of my own castle, and I wasn't alone. For forever, I wasn't alone.

I should like it that way. But something felt off. Wrong. Abysmally wrong. I was claiming a kill that wasn't mine. It wasn't anybody's. #9 *was not mine.* I had made her mine, because I liked what I saw and what I felt, but that still didn't make her mine. How could I make her all mine?

Rage filled every inch of my body and I screamed. Screamed out to the shadows in the dark. I wanted to make sure they heard. That they felt the rush and the onslaught of the anger as it left my body. Stunted and choked on my lips, it pushed me to swallow it whole once again. I wanted to vomit it up. To force it up and purge it from my rotted gut. But it wouldn't come.

Swallow it, Johnny. It's yours. Swallow it up, nice and good.

And I did.

Good boy, Johnny. Good boy.

I shot up and closed the box without another glance at the treasures inside. They made me sick now. Sick and so, so angry.

What are you going to do then, Johnny?

Nothing.

What are you going to do?

Nothing!

What the hell are you going to do, Johnny?

"Nothing!" I screamed into the darkness.

The darkness laughed back at me. Gagged and choked and hissed in its own pleasure. I stared at it hard, and it stared back at me.

"Nothing! Nothing! Nothing!" I yelled again and again.

Bam! Bam! Bam!

Someone pounded on the wall in the apartment next to me. I could hear them shouting back at me, telling me to shut up. I did and sat there trembling in the dark, staring down at that damn box. Slowly, warily, I opened it again. I could hear the tremulous sigh of those inside hit the air in a constipated hiss, choking on its own foul taste. I sighed with them, as I peered down into the box. There was my whole world, as incomplete and jagged as the black, beating heart within my heaving chest.

Bom-Bom. Bom-Bom. Bom-Bom!

Yeah, it did its job. It kept me alive, but it wasn't really alive. It didn't love, didn't fear, didn't feel. That's how it was with this box. It couldn't give me what the living girl, the flesh and the blood could give. Memories weren't the real thing. They would never—could never be.

So, Johnny? So, what does that mean?

I stared into the darkness, no longer trembling or afraid. Just hungry. Oh, so very hungry.

"It means," I said in a hissing whisper, "I need more."

I laughed. And the darkness laughed with me.

16 HAPPY HELL

Christmas came and went, wrapped in a blanket of heavy snow. It kept me from going on the prowl, despite my hunger. The good ones wouldn't come out in weather like that, and besides the holiday kept everyone inside celebrating and making their own merry love. I was left out of all that, all the cheer and the magic of the season. I hadn't celebrated anything conventional and traditional for ages. All that happiness didn't sit right with me. This time of year made me sick to my stomach. Into my month-long state of funk, I would go, not to be brought out until the sun peeked out on frosty January.

I spent the holidays sitting half-naked in my bed, channel surfing and eating my way through the China Dragon's three-page menu. I told myself I was having fun. But who was I kidding? I was miserable— miserable and hungry. There was nothing that would satisfy the biting ache in my stomach. Nothing but a sharp object and flesh to cut.

Blood was what I wanted for Christmas. Blood was the only present that would fill me with delight and fulfill my desire. It haunted my dreams instead of frolicking sugar plum fairies. Give me blood, not an endless supply of fake happiness and goodwill toward all men.

Drinking was about the only thing that distracted me from the crappiness of this Christmas. By 10 A.M. on Christmas morning, as the parade blasted across my television screen, I was as drunk as I could be, given that nothing was open that day and my supplies were already low. When it was gone, I closed my eyes and didn't wake up until late December 26th.

I decided to crawl out of my cocoon and wander out into the world. The snow had finally stopped, and the splendor of the holiday was over, at least until New Year's Eve reared its ugly head. Stepping out into the cold, I took a moment to breathe in the crisp afternoon air. There were a few people out, scattered here and there in the snow. Laughter and voices filled the light and frosty air, following me as I made my way down the street.

Something else was following me. Or I should say someone. I knew he was there long before he was in my eyeline. One of the cops that had paid me a visit was scooting his way along the sidewalk opposite me. Not looking my way. Not a hint that he was following me. But I knew, I could sense, that his radar was up. He was here just in case there was something worth seeing.

I glanced quickly toward him and caught him looking back at me. I wiped the look of recognition right off my face and pretended I didn't know him. I nodded his way with a casual half-smile and went about my business. Only my business was to lose him the first chance I had.

Twenty minutes later, I stood at an intersection, my sneakers balancing on the edge of the sidewalk, unsure of where to head next. There was no sight of Mr. Cop in any direction. I breathed a sigh of ready relief and waited to cross the street. The light hadn't turned red yet, and I stared into the coming traffic as it sped past.

Close call, kid. Keep your head up and stay—

A young woman stepped up next to me and everything else went away. She was beautiful from what little I could see of her in her bundle of winterwear. Her fur-lined hat framed her round and dark face. Her makeup was brightly colored, and it sparkled in the sunlight. There was a smile perfectly positioned on her red lips. I couldn't help but look at every inch of that face.

Until she caught me looking.

Her smile got wider as she turned to me. I chuckled a bit, my cheeks blushing right on cue. Shy boy, she must think. Shy but sweet.

You have no idea, girl.

"Hi," she said. The sunlight framed her like a halo.

I was getting ready to say something cunning and coy.

"Hello, Mr. Borden."

The sound of my name made me turn. And there he was. Mr. Cop. I turned back to the girl, only to find her gone. I watched her beautiful form disappear around a snowy corner.

Damn it.

Back to the cop. I didn't know his name—

"Hello. Sorry, I didn't catch your name last time we met." Insert plastic smile.

The cop smiled back; a cautious, empty smile that he must use just for professional purposes. "Detective Johnson."

Ah, "Detective Johnson", was it? Surely, we should be on a first name basis by now. After all he was looking for a killer and I was on his radar. He should at least try and make friends. Lighten the mood a bit. Maybe, just maybe, I would be a little more forthcoming with information. I could feed him a few more tidbits about my buddy Dan, if he would only play nice.

"How are you, Detective Johnson? What brings you out this way?" I made a point of emphasizing his stupid-ass name. Just so he knew that I had heard it.

"You, actually, Mr. Borden," he said, still with that forced smile. "I understand that you had an altercation at your workplace with Mr. Dan Wright."

Now, how would he know about that, unless good

old Dan let it slip? Was he trying to point a slippery finger at me now? Get these cops looking in my direction for once instead of his? But I could play my own games, Detective Johnson.

I put on my best face full of concern and proclaimed, "Dan's really gone off the deep end lately. He's not showing up for work and he's just paranoid all the time. He's talked about some pretty creepy shit, Detective. Let me tell you. Scared all of us half to death."

Detective Johnson looked alert now and highly intrigued. "What kinds of things was he telling you?"

I gave a dramatic pause before I said, "He talked one time about his dreams. Dark dreams. Dreams of blood and bodies. He seemed afraid as he was talking that these dreams would become real for him. When he came to work before the holidays, we were all surprised to see him. And then when he flew at me like that, I don't know, sir. I just don't know what's in his head these days."

Detective Johnson nodded, his mouth pursing in a grim line.

"I see."

He was quiet for a moment. I watched his eyes, waiting to see that spark of realization that I knew was coming. And—there it was. He was on the right track now. The track I wanted him on. Far, far away from me. He gave me one final fake smile. I returned it with my own. A farce we were both playing in this dangerous game.

One final nod and he said, "Thank you, Mr. Borden. Thank you for your time. I won't keep you. Have a good evening."

He walked away without another word. I breathed a heavy sigh as I watched him walk down the street.

"Happy New Year, Detective Johnson!" I called back just for laughs.

He turned back with a half-smile and then he was

gone.

That was a close call, boy. A close call.

"Yeah, yeah, yeah," I grumbled under my breath as I headed across the street.

17 Extreme Close-Ups and Close Calls

I had been parked at that 7-Eleven for over an hour. I was waiting for the cashier to get off work. She was alright, kind of pretty, kind of not. But good enough. She wasn't expecting me, wasn't waiting for me. But I was waiting for her.

She had smiled at me casually as I paid for my gas, her bubble gum pink lip gloss popping as her lips upturned. Her eyes were brown. Nothing special. Just plain old brown. They didn't sparkle or shine like Julianna's eyes. In fact, they were really a dull sort of brown, but they looked kind. Not Julianna kind—not invite me to her house and share her drugs kind. But still, they were kind. She also didn't look like the sort that would off herself at the first chance she had. She was safe—predictable. That was good enough for me.

After I paid for my gas, I pulled my car just out of her sight, and I waited. An hour later, she still hadn't gotten off work. I had watched her replacement for the evening shuffle inside. He was a chubby young teenager who looked infatuated over this mediocre girl of mine. Tongue out, eyes wide, sweaty-pitted love for her. I couldn't have that.

I was about to pull my car back up to the front and march inside to save her from the pining and prodding of this stupid kid, when I saw her reach under the counter for her purse. She smiled—politely—she obviously wasn't interested in this pizza-faced boy. She awkwardly waved to the kid right before she pushed open the door.

Ding!

Hello, beautiful.

Well, maybe not. She was still dressed in her uniform shirt, but I could at least see all of her now. I'd only seen the top half from my view on the other side of the store counter. What I'd seen in the store wasn't bad but seeing all of her now—sheesh! No hips and bony legs. She had on a short, short skirt despite the cold, showing off what she didn't have, and nobody wanted to see. I nearly turned my car around right then and there, but my body was already geared up for a kill. I couldn't disappoint myself. Not now. After #9, I was counting on this kill to cleanse me from that rottenness. If it didn't, I planned to just keep killing and killing and killing until it did.

I decided that she would do. She was nothing like my mother. Nothing like Julianna. She was her own black hole of hopeful anticipation and hungry chaos, and that I craved. Yeah, she might not be the *one* (no one could be now), but she would do.

I was about to pull up beside her when an obnoxious car horn sounded behind me. A sedan whipped in front of me and parked next to the sidewalk where she stood. I squinted in the collecting dark and couldn't believe my eyes. There was Dan. Work Dan. Picking up my date with destiny. She must be his date for the night.

Well, well, well. Mr. Dan must be throwing caution to the wind just for a little fun tonight.

Damn it.

She giggled loudly as she hopped into his car. And then he saw me. I swear he saw me. Our eyes pierced each other's in the dark. I expected him to look shocked or angry. Instead, he smiled as they sped off into the night. And I was left in their dust, wondering what the hell had just happened.

I drove around for hours. Radio blaring. Windows

down, despite the freezing cold. I wanted to freeze. To cool off the anger that was blazing full blast from every pore of my body. Let the cold wash over me and wash it all away. If that was even possible.

Tired of the nightscape of the city, I started down the backroads, heading out of town. Down, down, down, until a dark and lonely country road was all there was. Here, I could breathe. Deep breaths in. Deep breaths—

In the darkness up ahead, something caught my eye. It was almost as dark as the darkness itself. I drove slowly toward it, turning on my brights.

Bam!

There she was, that girl from the 7-11. She looked a little mussed and shaken. One of her shoes was missing and she hobbled down the gravel road, ignoring my approach. I pulled up next to her. She still clung to her purse as she pushed her frizzy blonde hair away from her face. Her cheeks were already pink from the frigid cold. I could see her rubbing her hands together to keep them warm. I bet she was regretting that short, short skirt now.

Believe me, we all were.

I slid up beside her, driving slowly. The radio was playing a good song for once. Perfect for this midnight interlude. She didn't glance over at first, so I rolled my window down.

"Hey."

Real smooth, Johnny. Real smooth.

But it worked. She turned her head my way, and I saw that she'd been crying. Her mascara was running down her pale cheeks, her lips trembling, from crying or the cold, I didn't know. Still, she smiled at me. Obviously, she wasn't the overly cautious type, except when it came to that purse. She clung to it like it was her lifeline. I wasn't worried about that, though. Her smile was enough of an invitation for me.

"Hey. You came," she said.

Acting coy seemed off with the way she looked wandering down this empty road alone. I doubted it was genuine. Just another ploy to get what she wanted, I guessed. Whatever *that* might be. A ride, perhaps? Maybe, just maybe.

"You want a ride?" I said, smiling like an idiot back at her. The kind of idiot that a girl like that would trust.

She glanced at my old truck and gave me a funny smirk. She was amused, I could tell. My quick thinking and suave creativity had done the trick and won her over. Now, all she had to say was—

"Sure."

Good thinking, Johnny.

Maybe she'd tired of good old Dan, or maybe he'd gotten tired of her and dumped her off in the middle of nowhere. Regardless, she had no qualms about taking a ride with a stranger like me. She seemed excited even, like it was a strange and curious adventure that she was about to embark on.

Anything but, sweetheart.

She plopped onto my passenger seat and slammed the car door. Turning to me with a big smile, she flipped her hair out of her face and held out her hand to me.

"Name's Samantha," she said, sniffling a little and wiping her mascara away on her work shirt.

Fresh as a daisy now. Ready for you, Johnny.

Samantha. Damn. I didn't want her to have a name. At any rate, I didn't want to know it. Giving these girls a name meant they became more than just another pointless nothing, another body to claim. No, now she had a face and a life, a future and a past. She became alive in my brain, taking up a space of recollection reserved only for one. This wouldn't do, but it was too late. I knew it now.

Keep it impersonal. Don't engage.

"Hi, Samantha. That's a nice name. Pretty."

Not what I meant to say at all, but there it was, out there on the air. Taking up space and filling up fast. She smiled back, giggling just a little. Ugh. That laugh. It was nasal and snotty, full of raging innocence and naivete that made me want to vomit. The more I looked at her, however, the more it seemed like a show just for me. She wasn't innocent or stupid, but she wanted me to believe she was.

Play along, Johnny. Just—play along.

"Where can I take you?" I asked cordially, a smile as wide as the crescent moon in the velvety black sky outside. "Sky's the limit. And even that's negotiable."

Big smile.

Good, Johnny. Good boy.

Her smile was so wide now, it could have lifted off her face and floated away into the night. God, I was good. I even surprised myself sometimes. There was that giggle again. Ugh. Please, kill me now.

No. Kill her, now!

Right, kill her. Okay. I'm easy. I'll oblige.

I looked to her and gestured eagerly for her to give me an answer. She wiggled into my passenger seat with delight, glancing out of the window at the rising darkness. Though it had been hours since the moon had newly peered out of its star-studded bed, it felt like only a second since I had set out from my apartment.

"Where are you headed?" she asked.

Ah, an open question and an invitation to take her just about anywhere I wanted. She was ready and willing.

"The movie theater down on Sixth Street?" I offered.

Hair pushed back with a smile. "Sure. What's playing?"

I shrugged with a cute little dip towards her. "Does it really matter?"

She giggled again and shook her head

emphatically. "No, not really."

I slid back to my side of the truck. "Alright, then. To the theater."

I glanced over at her while she was looking. Her eyes were on the landscape speeding past her window. She quickly bored of this and pulled the visor down to take a peek at her reflection in its cracked mirror. It was too dark to see, so she dug through her purse and brought out a Zippo lighter. Flash! And the flame sparked just enough for her to see herself in the mirror. She wiped at her smeared mascara by the light of that lonely, fragile flame, making pretty little shadows on the dashboard. Not on this girl's face though. In the yellow glow of the shifting light, it was as if the last remnants of sun hadn't faded and fizzled out, painting a rosy glow across her freckled cheeks, her honey-brown eyes.

Whoa, whoa, whoa. What—are you into this girl? Johnny? Johnny!

I shook my head in answer. She didn't notice. Deep breath in. Deep breath out.

Focus, Johnny.

Focus, yeah. Focus. She wasn't even pretty. Not attractive really, not even her glitter-specked cheeks that enhanced her warm brown freckles. The combination lit up her face like a Christmas tree even in the light of that damn Zippo. It was—nice.

Johnny!

Whoa! I had to all but slap myself back to reality as I gripped the steering wheel tighter. My palms were sweaty and cold. I seriously needed to get a grip. What was this girl doing to me? Did she know what she was doing? Was this her trap, her defense mechanism to lure me away from my plans?

If it is, it's working. Stupid, stupid boy.

SNAP!

She flipped the lighter closed and the dark took over in the cab once again.

Just then, as my will began to waver, she turned back to me. This time she wasn't smiling. She was just looking—in that way that girls like to look at you when their minds are on anything but the night's plans. My plans. Right—my plans.

I cleared my throat and turned my eyes back to the road ahead. This should be easy. Why wasn't it easy?

Her. It was her. She was making me like this. And why? I didn't know. I just kept my eyes on the road. That was all I could do. I felt her slide closer to me. Slowly, slowly closer, until she was all but on my lap. I felt her hand slip down to my leg as her lips pressed against my ear.

"Take me to the stars," she whispered, and my stomach just dropped to the floor at my feet.

No, no, no!

The truck tires squealed as I swerved off onto a backroad that led to nowhere. She bounced off me and dropped back into her seat. Way, way away from me. She seemed startled as I stopped the car with a jolting screech at the end of the road. From what I could see from the stream of light beaming from the headlights, we were facing a thickly wooded area. Good. That was great. Perfect for—

I turned to her with the wildness of a wolf gleaming in my eyes. But I was startled out of whatever wildness I had. I saw that she wasn't afraid. Instead, I saw that purse of hers lying open on the seat beside her and a gun staring me in the face. She held it like a pro. She'd obviously done this before, or at least practiced for the occasion. Her eyes were wide, but not from fear. Rather it was from the delight and anticipation of whatever she had in mind to do with it. With me.

I opened my mouth to speak, and she cocked the gun. Her head tilted to the side. She was inspecting me and enjoying every minute of it. Every inch of me.

"If you brought me out here to kill me, you've got another thing coming," she said. Her voice never wavered. Her hands weren't shaking. Her aim was impeccable. She knew what she was doing, alright.

Damn.

I swallowed hard, gulping down the lump of acid stuck in my throat. It didn't go all the way down. Just sat heavy in my chest. I was starting to get sick to my stomach. This wasn't going to end well.

You've got that right.

The radio was playing softly. Late night oldies.

"I like this song," she said.

She turned it up full blast until the car rattled with the sound of the bass and the drums. The gun was still aimed at me, but she leaned in, grabbed my face, and kissed me hard. She sucked on my lips like she couldn't get enough. When she pulled away, she wasn't smiling. She didn't look satisfied.

"Gets me in the mood," she said, almost as an afterthought.

I slid away from her and the gun. "For what?" I asked timidly.

I was listing and almost sunk. She had undone me, and nothing was going to go according to plan from this moment on. I knew that much. She leaned back on the passenger door, her chest heaving breathlessly as she gave me a devilish grin.

"Say my name," she half-whispered.

"What?"

She leaned back further, her head against the window. She braced herself and aimed the gun at my head with a flicker of delight in her impish eyes.

"Say my freaking name."

I stumbled to form the word, the sounds tripping on my tongue like lead scraping a sidewalk. But I got it out.

"Samantha."

She smiled like it was her own private joke. Giggling like a schoolgirl, she rolled the window down all the way.

"Phew!" she exclaimed. "That's better. I can't stand heat."

She fanned herself with the hand that held the gun.

I flinched and moved just an inch and the gun was back in my face. She looked determined, her features set in a decided and hungry expression. She smiled, but it was no longer innocent and naïve. No, she knew what the hell she was doing and what she wanted.

That's when she said, "You do this all the time?"

I shook my head. Like I was really going to tell her the truth about me. Somehow, though, in that silent way she inspected me, I felt like she could see it. Like she already knew.

"Don't mess with me—"

"Johnny." I said quietly.

She nodded.

"Johnny—that's cute. Like you're some kind of nerd boy who bags groceries at the local Piggly Wiggly."

I blushed. Not from embarrassment, although there was plenty of that. No, this was from anger. She had pegged me as some kind of loser.

"But you're really a hot shot hot boy that gets his kicks knocking off innocent young girls on backroads."

Maybe she did have me pegged right after all. Against my better judgment, I shrugged guiltily with a smile. She looked at me, long and hard, gun still aimed, and slowly, she smiled back. It was an awkward shared moment, delightful in its own strange way as I connected with this crazy girl.

Finally, she pulled back her gun hand, resting it on her thigh with the gun aimed at the ceiling. She looked amused. I was curiously amused myself. I cocked my head to the side as I looked her over. She let me look, enjoying the attention and the curiosity.

"Like what you see?" she said in a seductive whisper.

She ran the barrel of the gun across the bare skin

of her chest, her eyes on me. Her hand was on the trigger, ready to pull it.

"Tell me I'm pretty," she said softly.

She's bat-shit crazy.

Quiet, I can handle this alone. I didn't answer quick enough, and she looked a little hurt and angry.

"It's okay if you don't. I know you're not going to kill me anyways. Not when I can blow your family jewels halfway to hell and leave you to bleed like a stuck pig here in this truck."

Fair enough.

"Not really my taste, but I'm not complaining."

She wasn't hurt by that. Instead, she laughed. I watched nervously as the gun flailed about wildly in her hand, fearful for its aim. I put a hand down subtly to cover my valuables just in case she wasn't kidding. She noticed and smiled.

"What is your taste, then? Hot girls? Big boobs, big ass, and legs for miles?"

It was getting scary how spot on her guesses were now. I blushed again, this time from embarrassment. She made it sound so cheap, so degrading. It made me feel dirty and disposable, something that I didn't like and hadn't ever felt before.

I noticed she was watching me closely. I felt like a frame from a movie scene, one of those extreme close-ups that fill up the entire screen. Revealing everything, every minute and miniscule movement and expression. Every thought seems transparent. Every emotion is as plain as if it were written on a page of burning notebook paper. There for a second, as long as the frame holds steady on the screen, and then, it's gone. Rubbed out. Smoked out and melted away.

I had never had anyone look at me that way, picking me clean and poking my remnants into a microscope to get an even better image. I had always been a shadow and that's how I liked it. Until now. I liked the way she looked at me. I liked the way it made me feel—exposed and raw—because it made me *feel*.

She seemed neither angry nor hurt by my silent admission. She seemed void of any opinion about me at the moment. She just sat looking.

"Figures," she mumbled. "But I bet you're never satisfied. Always hungry. Always something better coming if you just keep looking."

I had to get that freaking gun away from her. I inched closer to her. She let me, the gun still playing around her chest. She licked her lips with a devilish smile. So, I slid a little closer. Our legs were touching, the bare skin of her bony legs against the skin peeking out from the ratty holes of my worn jeans.

"Are you?" I took the leap and asked.

It sparked a flame that burned a sultry red in her eyes. It was dangerous, yeah, but it was beautiful. It was a dare meant for me.

Take me on. Go on and try it. But careful, I bite.

Her mouth opened just slightly as she exhaled her answer, "Never."

Her lips were tantalizing as she spoke, glossy and pink, and permanently set in a pout I couldn't ignore. They slid into an easy smile that sent shivers down my spine. I couldn't resist, and so, I kissed her. Long and slow.

I felt her body fall into mine, easing into the kiss. She closed her eyes, sighing passionately into my open mouth. I kept my eyes open, staring down her gun hand. Watching as her finger slowly pulled away from the trigger. Slowly, slowly, her hand loosened its white-knuckled grip on the gun.

Now, boy. Now!

Slowly, slowly, I raised my arm as if to wrap it around her body. She leaned in closer to let me. And that's when I grabbed for the gun. She let out a scream as she tried to grab it from me, but I swiped it out of her reach and backed up to the door. In a flash, I had aimed the gun.

Bang! Bang!

I expected to see red, but at first there was nothing. She stared at me. Her very plain brown eyes stared me down, her over-glossed mouth hanging open dumbly as a gurgling sound erupted from her throat. She didn't move, her breathing sporadic and congested. And then, with a heavy sigh, her head hung low, hiding her eyes, and I saw a cherry-red stain growing at the edge of her side.

I sighed with relief. It was quiet, so quiet in the truck. In the night. There was not a sound from her. Not a flinch of movement. She was dead.

I dropped the gun onto the passenger side floor and turned back to turn on the car. The engine vroomed to life, filling the silence with the sweet, sweet sound of white noise. Outside my windshield, the night was in full swing, the stars sprinkling the blackness like tiny spotlights. All of them bright. All of them beaming down on me to show the world what I had done. I felt like there were a million eyes on me. Judging me. Screaming so loudly that I was a killer.

Well, kid, you are.

That didn't sit well with me. Frantically, I put the truck in park and jumped out. I walked around to the other side of the truck, taking a deep breath. My hands were shaking. My whole body was shaking wildly. I stared at her frizzy blonde hair smushed against my window for a long while, hesitant to open the door.

Come on, boy. Get on with it. Someone might see.

Someone had seen. A million of them up there in the sky. And whatever else was up there. The whole universe. God maybe.

Easy there, partner. Get your head back in the game.

Get back in the game. Right. I ripped the car door open, and she came tumbling out onto me, her limp body collapsing into my arms. I was lucky I caught her before she hit the ground. She wasn't cold or rigid yet; her limbs were still pliable, which helped as I dragged her to the back of the truck. Popping open the tailgate, I propped up her body against it as I jumped into the truck bed. Crouching down, I grabbed her underneath her arms and pulled her up into the bed.

Plop! And she was in and ready for a ride.

Standing in the truck bed, I took a moment to catch my breath. My eyes wandered from her dead body to the stars up above. They were watching, I could feel it. But they were also lovely to look at. Dangerous but beautiful. As I watched, a shooting star streaked across the sky. I followed it until it disappeared behind the wall of forest in front of the truck. My headlights were still on, beaming out ahead into the night. That's when I noticed a dirt path up ahead, just big enough for my truck to pass through.

Perfect. Nice eye, Johnny.

Maybe I was wrong. Maybe the stars were on my side. Maybe they'd seen everything and liked what they saw. I was, after all, putting on a pretty good show.

I hopped back into my truck and got it started. I eased the vehicle slowly down the dirt path. It wasn't really a road and my truck barely fit it, and even then, the brush and twigs were scraping against its sides. There was nothing around me but trees and darkness. It was ghostly and eerily quiet, a fog rolling in just in time to make it creepy. I took a deep breath and kept going. I had to find the perfect spot to dump her.

About a half mile into the woods, I was starting to get lost. Finally, I found it, the spot for her. I stopped my truck, keeping the headlights beaming on the area I had picked. I got out of the truck and inspected it. A little way from the path, there was a dip and a short fall that led into a hollow. It was deep, dark, and foggy. I couldn't see where it led to, but it would have to do. I was tired of driving in these godforsaken woods. It would take me forever to find my way out of them.

I walked around to the back of the truck, ready to finish this once and for all.

"You didn't actually think that would work, right?"

I nearly jumped out of my skin. There she was—Samantha—sitting up and leaning against the back of the truck. She was bloody but very, very alive. And very, very pissed. The full moon light was harsh on her pale features and a little blood had smeared across her cheek into her hair, where she must have tugged the strands away from her eyes.

I was speechless, so she filled the awkward, eerie silence.

"Really, Johnny. I was expecting much more than this." She gestured toward her side. The bloody patch was bigger, but it wasn't bleeding profusely. I must have just nicked her with the bullet. Damn it.

"Damn it," I whispered.

She looked even more angry, tilting her head to the side with a crazily amused expression.

"Yeah, Johnny. Damn it. This was my work shirt. Now I have to pay for another one."

"You can soak it, the blood will come out in the wash," I had no idea why I was helping the woman I had just killed. Or thought I had killed.

She slapped her hands down in her lap with a huff.

"Will soaking it fix where you shredded it with MY freaking bullet?"

"I-I'm sorry..." I muttered. My heart was beating hard and loud in my ears, like a freight train or a twister or a bomb. It was deafening and I couldn't think straight. This woman was supposed to be dead. She was supposed to be dead.

Samantha was supposed to be dead!

She scrambled to her feet, wincing a little and cussing under her breath. She dusted off her short, short skirt, and then, she looked at me, her eyes gleaming eerily in the moonlight. She stood there, hands on hips, tapping her foot on the metal truck bed.

"My father is going to kill me," she muttered. I don't think she thought I would hear her, but of course, I did.

My head was alert now and I was scared.

"Your father? Wait! How old are you?" I demanded. My voice echoed on the frigid, frosty air.

She turned to me with a grimace as she smoothed out her ruined shirt and hopped down out of the truck. She winced and whined a little as she hit the ground, clutching her side, but then she whipped around to me. Eyes narrowed. Fists clenched.

"Who cares how old I am," she said. "You're old enough to know better."

With that she began to march her way into the darkness of the dirt path. Her sneakers crunched loudly on the gritty road, grinding at my last nerve.

Had enough, Johnny?

I screamed. She stopped. She turned back with less enthusiasm, her pale face sneering at me. I wasn't expecting that. I wasn't expecting any of this.

"I-I..."

Ugh, I needed to pull it together. Seriously.

"I'll take you home."

She huffed and puffed until her face had some color again. "How the hell am I supposed to go home like this? What am I supposed to say? Hmm? 'Gee, Mom and Dad, I guess you were right when you told me not to take rides from strangers, because some cute guy just *shot* me!'"

She wriggled and writhed in her anger, her toes pointing inward as she stood awkwardly trying to emote. But being young and stupid, feelings don't always come naturally like they should. Instead, you end up in a temper tantrum like a two-year-old, which was where she was at right now. It was kind of cute actually.

She caught me staring and glared at me with that

childish pout. I couldn't help myself. I laughed. And she screamed. Then, it was silent, both of us looking at each other with the feeling of "What the hell do we do now?"

Finally, I said, "Where do you want to go?"

Back in my car and out of that damn forest, we were on the road again. Samantha was back in the seat beside me, rather quiet as she brooded. She had rolled the window down all the way, letting out all the warm air and replacing it with damp coolness like a freezer door had been left open. She hung her head out of the window, letting the cold air sweep up her blonde frizz and send it flying into the night. Then she closed her eyes.

We were back in the heart of the city now and she pulled her face back into the car, folding her arms tightly around her chest with a huffing sound. She looked young. Very young. So, I had to ask—

"Just how old are you?"

No answer. So, I probed a bit more.

"Look, I don't want to get arrested for picking you up, if you know what I mean?"

She mulled it over in her head for a minute. "Nineteen. I'm nineteen."

I let out a very loud sigh of relief that made her turn with a look of disgust.

"Are you sure?" I asked, a bit shaky.

She seemed offended by the question. "Am I sure of what? Am I sure I'm nineteen? Yes, I believe if you check my driver's license you will see that I am clearly nineteen years old."

Quiet, and then— "How old are you?"

She was turning the tables on me, pinning me down to questions I didn't want to answer. I didn't want to make it personal. Not on any level. I just needed to get her home. I couldn't let anyone see her with me.

"How old are you, Johnny?" she demanded.

"Twenty-six. I'm twenty-six."

This was bad. This was very bad. I was a grown-ass adult, and she was just a kid. Old enough to make it legal, but young enough to know better. This was bad. This was very bad.

"Where do you live, Johnny?"

I laughed out of nervousness. But when I looked in her eyes, I knew she wasn't joking around with me. She meant business.

"Just a few streets over."

She pouted a little longer, wincing with every bump on the road, every jostling turn I made with the truck. Every bump on the road that I purposely drove over and every turn I whipped through just to watch her squirm. No one said I couldn't have a little fun, especially after her charade in the woods.

"Take me home," she finally said.

"Alright, where do you live?"

Looking me straight in the eye, she said, "Take me to your home."

I hesitated a moment too long.

"You still owe me a good time," she added.

I owed her a bullet in the head, like I had wanted to do back there. Instead, I had chickened out and now I was stuck with her. This had turned into the night from hell. What the hell was I supposed to do with this teenager now? If I let her go and dumped her out on the street, she'd just go to the cops and blab all about her little adventure in the bed of my truck. They would know all about this night and all about me.

I couldn't let that happen. So, to my home we would go. I prayed to the stars, to the universe, to whatever God was up there in that spatial void that this night wouldn't be the end and that she wouldn't be the death of me.

18 TUBS OF GUTS (OR TUBS AND GUTS)

I took Samantha home with me. By the time we got inside, I was in a foggy funk that was getting heavier and thicker all the time. I didn't bother showing her around. In fact, I didn't speak to her at all. I just threw down my jacket, pulled off my shirt, and collapsed onto my bed in the middle of the room.

I was nearly out when I felt my shoes being tugged and pulled off my feet. I heard them tumble to the floor. A thin-framed shadow stood over me, unrecognizable in the darkness. I shooed it away with a grunt and a groan, turning my head so I couldn't see it.

"I was good, Mama. Honest. I was good," I muttered, but the words, my voice, seemed alien and strange. Small and childlike.

The shadow came closer, and I flinched, wrapping my arms about myself defensively. "Please, not again," I whispered, trembling all over.

The strange shadow complied and came no nearer. In seconds, it had faded away into the darkness and was gone. I was alone. Utterly alone. Not even the shadows and the darkness wanted me. With a groan, I curled up in a ball, avoiding the touch of the cold air and the hiss of the shadows lain heavy in every corner.

I lay there in a semi-conscious state, fading in and out, and dreaming all the while. Dreaming of Julianna. And my mother. I could feel them hovering over me, watching. Always watching and whispering in my ear. I wouldn't let them have me this time. I wouldn't let them in. I shut my eyes tight, so tight my head ached, and stars danced around my eyelids. But I managed to fall fitfully asleep.

***

"Johnny—"
I could hear the water sloshing and sputtering and spewing before I even opened my eyes. It was coming from the bathroom. It was the tub faucet. Something squeaked and clanged against the sides of the tub. The sound gutted me, ripped out every inch of comfort my delirium had had, leaving only that primal fear. The fear of blood and flesh. Rotten, all rotten.
"Johnny—"
I crawled off the bed and scrambled to my stocking feet. The floor was ice cold. The air itself was freezing and I trembled as I tiptoed my way toward the closed bathroom door. Warily, I brought a shaking hand to the door and laid it there. I pressed it in hard, as if I had the power to split the door in two with the power of my fingertips. I quelled a scream upon my lips, biting my tongue until I could taste a tinge of blood.
I could hear the water still running, loud and rushing. I went to open the door. What would I find? Julianna? My mother—oh god, my mother?
Johnny, open the door. Open the door, Johnny.
So, I did. It creaked open slowly, like a present in my hands, opening and revealing what lay inside. But I already knew it was nothing I wanted.
I was immediately blinded by the harsh fluorescent light of the bathroom. I took a step in and regretted it. There in the tub full of water was Samantha. She lay with her head cocked to the side. Her hair was wet, and her body didn't move except to slosh up and down in the water.
"Julianna..." The name tripped off my tongue like a

shard of glass cutting deep. A tear rolled down my cheek as I expelled the contents of my stomach onto the cool white tile below. I slipped to the floor, fading fast. Right before I did, I saw her turn toward me. She looked me in the eye with curiosity and fear. Then, there was nothing.

19 ABOUT WHAT HAPPENED TONIGHT (OR NOT #10)

I woke up to the smell of something rancid and burnt. It played on my nostrils and burned like an acid bath. Before I had even opened my eyes, I could hear the clanging sound of a pan on the stove and the hiss and sizzle of something cooking. Or burning from the smell of it. Another loud *clang* and—

"Damn it."

My eyes popped open. I was sprawled out like a dead man on my bed. I'd given the girl my futon for the night. I glanced over to it and found the contents of her purse strewn all over the couch turned bed. The blanket I had given her was bunched in a corner of it, stained with her blood.

I dragged myself to a sitting position, just in time to see the girl, Samantha, about to set fire to my whole damn kitchenette. Flames burst from the pan and ran up the wall. In an instant, the smoke alarm was blaring. I jumped to my feet and ran to the stove. The girl just stood there, staring at the flames like some dumb idiot, frozen in both fascination and fear. I pushed her aside and reached under the sink to grab the fire extinguisher. Within seconds I had the fire out. Breathless and angry, I looked at the damage. I'd have to call the super. There went my security deposit.

Bam!

The smoke alarm smashed to the floor. At least it was quiet now. I turned to find the girl standing over it with a broom in her hand. She smiled a quirky "sorry" smile and shrugged her shoulders. She was dressed in one of my white tank tops, which she had dressed up by tying it in a knot just above her belly button. It showed off her hipless waist and the handy dandy bandaging she'd done on her wound in the middle of the night. The get-up made her look even more like a child, which didn't sit right with me, and I turned away.

I looked down to see the pan she had set on fire. She was making grilled cheese sandwiches. There were some burnt ones resting on a plate next to the stove. Geez, she *was* like a little kid. Wrapping the handle in the bottom of my t-shirt, I grabbed the smoking hot pan off the stove. It was still scorching hot though. As fast as I could, I dropped into the sink. As I ran the cold water over it, the steam saturated the air.

"Hope you're hungry."

Through the smoke and steam, I saw her standing in front of me, staring me down with a look I couldn't explain and didn't understand. She was still holding the melted spatula she had used. She gripped it tightly, as if she could use it as a weapon, if it came to that with me. I almost laughed, but I didn't. This chick was crazy, and I didn't want to piss her off. Instead, I just nodded.

She scrambled behind me and grabbed the plate of sandwiches. She grabbed two glasses topped off with milk from the counter. Balancing everything in her hands, and wincing just a little, she took it all to the coffee table and set it up like a proper dinner. Napkins, knives, and forks. Everything. All laid out so neatly.

She sat on the futon in front of the coffee table, smoothing out her skirt as she waited for me. Warily, I sat down on the bed, sitting just in front of her with the table between us (for which I was grateful). I wanted as much distance between that girl and me as possible.

Noticing that I didn't help myself, she grabbed a steaming hot sandwich and plopped it on the plate in front of me. I stared down at it, at the whole set up. When I looked up at her, she seemed to be eagerly awaiting some kind of something from me.

"Where'd you get the bread and the milk? I don't have—"

"I went to the convenience store down the street a couple hours ago," she said through a globby mouthful of sandwich.

She must have been hungry. There was a hair in mine. One of hers. It was peeking out of the blackened crusty edge, just staring back at me. I tried not to make a face of disgust in front of her. I swallowed hard.

"Where'd you get the money?"

She was quiet, conveniently busy with a mouthful of food, which she seemed to chew for a very long time.

"I found some money in your wallet," she said quietly as she swallowed hard.

She avoided my eyes and snatched her milk off the table. It was gone in one gulp, a perfect milk mustache rimming her thin lips. No longer bubble-gum pink. No longer glossed and shining.

"So, you stole from me?"

"No!" The girl was quick to exclaim as she brushed crumbs off her skirt. "Borrowed. Anyway, it was for you. You get to eat it and keep what's left over. I just , did you a favor."

She motioned with her eyes for me to try a piece of my sandwich. As if that would somehow release this tension in the room and make everything better in her eyes.

So, I did. I picked up the whole sandwich, hair and all, and ate it. I crammed it into my face like there was no tomorrow and swallowed it down with my glass of milk. The milk was warm, and my stomach churned. I swallowed hard and looked back at her.

"Good," I said, knowing what I had just eaten was going to come back to haunt me very, very soon.

Samantha smiled, pleased with herself. She fiddled with her knife, scraping it across her plate until it screeched, whined, and grated on my last nerve. I remembered the last few hours with this woman. Like a terribly long and drawn-out flashback in a movie, it replayed in my mind until I shivered with disgust and horror. As if she could read my thoughts, she stopped what she was doing, the knife still in hand.

"Johnny—"

I forgot she knew my name.

"About what happened tonight."

There it was. I waited. I was curious what she would have to say. Her eyes avoided my stare like the plague, and I wondered why she was suddenly so timid. That façade of innocence and cute naivete was back for a rerun. This time it was forced and rusty, like she had forgotten how to play her own.

"Who's Julianna?"

I wasn't expecting that. My head jolted back with the surprise of it. A tear rose to my eyes.

Johnny—

I turned toward the sound. The sound of my mother's voice. Of Julianna's sweet whisper. All melded into one horrendous call. I tried to ignore it. I blinked away the tears in my eyes and looked that girl dead in the eye.

"Why did you get in my truck?" I asked, leaning back against the wall.

Her eyes skated across my face, her pale cheeks beginning to flush. "It was dark. And..."

Now she had my attention and a half-smile crept up on my face.

"And?"

She went for her glass of milk, forgetting she had drained it dry a minute ago. Her antsy fingers fumbled around in her lap.

Then she looked at me, and said, "I only just started working at the store. This guy, Dan, he would come in a lot like you. He would always act real sweet to me, smile, and say all the right things. He didn't care how old I was. He wanted to be with me. Kept flirting with me at the counter and asked me out when my store manager wasn't looking. Finally, tonight I just said yes. He picked me up after work, and at first, everything was nice. He was a perfect gentleman. A little handsy. But what guy isn't?

"It got to be a little rough. A little too much. And I tried to tell him so, but he...he wouldn't stop. I remember catching a glimpse of myself in the window. I looked so scared. So deathly afraid and helpless. And I never wanted to feel like that. Not with him. Not with any man. So, I knew what I had to do.

"It was all so easy, really. He didn't even see me reach for the gun I knew he kept in his glove compartment. I grabbed it, aimed it and pop! His brains were splattered all over his damn precious car."

She giggled then. Her brown eyes flashed with a shade of black.

"I hit him on the head with my shoe. Broke the damn heel. You know, just to make sure he was really dead."

"Was he?" I asked.

"Oh, yeah. I know what dead looks like. And this was *dead* dead. Dead, like never coming back dead." She turned to me with a sweet smile that unnerved me. "And then, there you were. You appeared like a godsend just after I had scooted out of his car and slipped down that backroad. And then..."

"And then," I continued for her. "You tried to kill me."

She glared at me, "Well, obviously it didn't work, did it?"

I shrugged, surrendering. She got quiet then, so I said, "I didn't. I didn't see you. Or the gun. I was too busy looking at your face."

Her face lit up as if on cue. "What about my face?"

I shrugged again, feeling awkward. "It was pretty. But that's before I knew how old you were."

She blushed with a smile all the same. "You thought I was pretty?"

"Well, yeah. Before you tried to shoot me."

She grunted as she grabbed for another cheese sandwich, stuffing her face. She didn't care what I thought now. She had what she thought was my approval, my acceptance.

I wasn't hungry anymore. My stomach was sick to think of that man splattered and splayed out on his leather seats. This was bad. This was very, very bad. And here was bad, sitting casually on my worn-out futon, dressed up a like a pretty girl.

Oh, so she's pretty now?

"Shut up," I muttered.

"What?" she asked, looking confused.

I shook my head emphatically, my eyes drifting away. She let it go and went for another sandwich, but as her hand grazed the crusty sides of the blackened bread, she pulled back.

"Do you really kill people?" she asked softly, like a secret.

I smiled softly back at her, my head hanging to the side to look at her in a different light.

"Now what makes you think you know me?" I whispered.

She whispered back, her eyes wide, but not with fear. "When you looked at me, you had that same look in your eyes that my father has when he's hunting. That same wild, predatory hunger that can only be satisfied at the edge of a trigger."

I laughed at the fear in her eyes. The first I had seen of it the entire time I had been with her. She wasn't the type to frighten easily. I knew that just by looking at her. So, what was this? This fear I saw now so easily flickering in the brown of her eyes. I had seen that kind of fear so many times in the split second before metal met flesh, blood, and bone. It made me hungry, but I didn't want to be hungry for her. Not now.

I pushed up and off the bed with a smirk on my face. "Who says I would use a gun anyway?"

I turned my back on her.

"I don't care, you know."

I heard her say and turned back. The fear was gone, and she was serious. Dead serious.

"Your business is your business. Just like that guy is mine. And we don't have to talk about it anymore."

"Fair enough," I said with a nod of my head. I couldn't believe it. Dan, my good old Dan was dead as a doornail. Rotting in his precious sedan on a backroad somewhere. I was elated. My problem was solved. Happy, I was happy.

Until I realized—"But we still have the fact that there's a dead guy that *you* shot, and basically, I was the getaway driver."

She squinted at me and said, "You don't seem shocked or worried about him though."

"Yeah, well Dan deserved whatever he got this time."

Her eyes got wide. "You knew him?"

"He was on my tail. Figured me out. At least I think he did."

"So, you're happy he's dead?"

I laughed, a little too eagerly. A little too freely. "Yeah," I said smugly.

Bad for poor Dan, better for us.

Us? When did this become an "us" thing? There was no "us". There was only me and this stupid girl—

Samantha.

Stop saying her name. This—*girl*—was just in the way. I could kill her. I could kill her now and be done with the whole thing.

Instinctively, as if my body had already made up my mind for me, I grabbed for a knife on the counter that she had used for the sandwiches. I lunged for her with the dirty knife, but she didn't move. Didn't try to run. In fact, she didn't do anything. Just stared at me intensely as I ran toward her, screaming. The knife stopped just above her chest. Her breathing was normal, slow and steady, not frantic like my own. Not like it would be if she was afraid. Because she wasn't. Well, that was a disappointment.

"Why aren't you afraid?" I said soft and low.

She looked me dead in the eyes and whispered, "Because I know you won't kill me."

She was right. For some reason, I couldn't. Not yet. I lowered the knife to my side with a sigh of utter unrest. My body was geared for a kill; it was begging for it. But I couldn't give it what it wanted just now. And she knew that.

"So, you are a killer," she said, looking rather proud of herself that she had been proven right about me.

I tumbled down onto my bed, lying there sprawled out again. I didn't care if she was there or not. I hadn't asked for company.

"Yeah, well, so are you. So, we're even."

She was quiet for a moment. I closed my eyes.

"I can't go home."

I waited for it. I knew what was coming.

"Can I stay with you?"

I sighed heavily. "You owe me a favor."

"What?" she started.

I let my eyes turn to her with a look of annoyance and compliance. "There's something we have to do."

She smiled. And I smiled back, right before my stomach wrenched and churned, and I vomited up all that warm milk and burnt bread.

20 A BREAK-IN, A BREAK-UP AND A REUNION (ALL IN ONE NIGHT)

It was three in the morning. We were back in my truck, driving down every stupid backroad there was because *somebody* couldn't remember where she'd left the dead body of her date and his car. It was an over-the-top, souped-up Plymouth! How can you lose *that*? Regardless, there we were driving endlessly in awkward silence, as the clouds spit tiny flakes of snow and ice that crackled and tapped on the windshield.

It was cold and the truck's heat had fizzled out miles back. Samantha didn't seem to mind. From what I gathered; she liked the feel of the cold. Maybe it kept her alert and focused. I didn't know. But she rolled her window down and hung her head out to feel the air. I glanced her way and saw her open her mouth and stick her tongue out to catch the snow. Nestled in her lap was my box.

"Are you looking or not?" I demanded, a little snarkier than I had expected.

She whipped a fitful glance at me and stuck out her tongue.

"Yes, alright?! It's not my fault that every damn backroad looks the same!"

Suddenly she perked up in her seat, alert and watchful like a prairie dog. Her eyes got big, and she said, "Shh! This looks familiar."

I looked ahead the best that I could, but there was no car in sight. "Are you sure?" I asked.

She didn't look at me. She was focused and alert

now. Suddenly, she popped up in her seat, frantically pointing up ahead into the darkness.

"There! It's there."

"Where?"

She looked frustrated now. "You don't see it? It's right up there!" She hopped up and down in the seat, pointing with purpose.

Annoyed, I sat forward, peering into the dim headlight glow.

Well, what do you know? The girl is right.

There it was, Dan's cherry-red, souped-up Plymouth. It's custom paint job glaring in the night like a beacon that screamed, "Murder! Get your murder, right here!"

I slowed down and parked right in front of Dan's car. It was off to the side, mingled in with the waist-high weeds and brush that rattled and shook in the wind. It was silent in the truck then. We both stared down at the eerily dark car. She sank down deep into her seat, sighing heavily. She clung to my kill box like a treasure chest. I kept her gun tucked in my pants for safe keeping.

One glance at her and she nodded silently. She opened the car door and hopped out with my box. I followed her, and we walked to the driver's side of Dan's car. We stood there for a long moment, staring into the darkened car. In the light of my truck's high-beams, I could just make out Dan's body slumped over in the front seat. The moonlight shining through the windshield made his lifeless body look ghostly white.

Without a word, Samantha took a deep breath and opened Dan's door. I got a better look at him at that point.

Geez, that girl's a good shot.

She *was* a good shot. She'd managed to shoot him in the forehead. One and done, *bam!* And he was dead. Like graveyard dead. His brains and a bucketful of blood covered the back seat and the windows.

No more Dan.

I couldn't help but smile, and she saw that. Her face looked frightened, her eyes wide, but a hint of a smile crept across her pink lips. That was for me.

The girl gestured with an odd sort-of pleasure toward Dan's dead body. Her smile growing wider. "Will this fit in your little box?"

I laughed out loud. "Why? Do you want to keep him?"

She seemed startled at first, but she quickly chimed in with her own careful laughter. The awkwardness of the moment drifted up and away like the wisps of cloud from our mouths as we breathed. A collective sigh and a hush fell over us. We looked at one another by the light of my truck. It was almost magical—*almost*—a dreamlike state of nirvana that hung in the air between us.

It lasted only a brief instant before she said, "You got the gun?"

I woke from my happy stupor and retrieved the gun from my pants. I went to hand it to her, but I stopped, eyeing her with a quizzical look.

"You know what you're doing?"

She huffed, her shoulders sagging. She held her hand out for the gun. "Of course, I do! I'm the one that shot him. I should know how to make it look like a suicide."

The girl grabbed the gun out of my hand and turned around to face the body. All that bravado and all that loud-mouthed sass went out the window. She leaned in over the body, crawling over Dan on her knees. By the time she hovered over his face, she was covered in bloody splotches and brain matter. Realizing this, she gagged violently.

I'd had enough and marched around to the passenger side, threw open the door, and grabbed the gun out of her shaking hand.

"Give me that!" I whispered loudly, as if even the

stars could hear in this deep quiet. "You talk a big game, but you see a little blood and brains, and you're useless."

"And you aren't, I suppose?" She countered, before she realized what she'd said. She blushed with embarrassment and said, "Oh."

Then, she vomited on my sneakers. They were my favorite sneakers too. She was going to owe me big time for this.

I wiped the gun free of prints with my t-shirt and wrapped the handle in it. Carefully, I lifted up Dan's rigid and icy cold hand and did my best to get it to grip the gun. I got his prints all over that sucker. Satisfied, I plopped the gun on the car floor and turned to Samantha with a look of pride. But she wasn't impressed, just scared.

Frustrated, I said curtly, "Get the box."

Samantha's body eclipsed the car light and framed her face like a halo. She seemed otherworldly in that moment, a touch of heaven or an ember of hell. Either way, it frightened me. Not because I feared either one, but because at that moment, she was both to me.

Reluctantly, she did as she was told. She grabbed up my box from the ground and brought it carefully over to me tucked neatly under her arm. She clung to it like I'd seen her cling to that gun of hers. The gun that was now going to frame this loser for everything I'd done. Everything that this girl had done too. Good old Dan had become the perfect scapegoat for both of us. And all because he wanted a little love on a Friday night.

Good old Dan. Thanks for your service.

I placed my box of goodies on the seat beside him. Inside, I had put newspaper clippings of almost all of my kills. The ones the police had kept tabs on. I thought about keeping Julianna's name tag. I opened the box one last time to take one final look at it, at all my treasures. I hated letting them go. I hated the idea of them in the hands of the police who would discard them with disgust in a locked, sealed room forever and ever. All my efforts hidden away. What a waste! But there they lay next to Dan's bloody body. A wasted collection of dreams.

I felt eyes on me and looked up to see the girl staring straight at me. She came around to my side of the car. We stared at the mess we had made together until the silence became unbearable.

Then she said, "Let's go back."

And that was it. I headed for my truck, and she trailed behind. I waited to start my truck until she hopped in, looking chipper for someone who had just been attacked and had shot the son of a bitch. Granted, he had deserved everything he got, but still, it seemed strange to drive back down that dark road with her smiling that way. Strange, but then again, everything had been strange on this bloody night from hell.

21 FAREWELL AND FORGET YOU

The sun was coming up now and we were still driving. We were both quiet as we reached the city limits and stopped just at the sign.

GOODBYE. SEE YOU NEXT TIME.

Yeah, right. See you when I'm rotting in hell.

Samantha tilted her head to the side, looking perturbed at the sign. "It'll be a cold day in hell before I miss this place."

I looked at her and she looked at me. We didn't have to say anything. We had both already decided that the city limits weren't far enough. We had to go further, go as far as we could go.

So, I put the car in drive and skidded forward, leaving perfect black skid marks where we had been. It wasn't the only mark we had left on that city, but it was the one that gave me the most pleasure. It was a permanent mark in a way that my kills could never be. Those were hidden away and secret, but this—this was something that everyone would see and know that we had been here.

As we sped off onto the open highway, Samantha opened her window all the way and stuck her upper body out of the window. Raising her hands in the air, she screamed.

"Goodbye! Farewell assholes and forget you!"

Yeah, goodbye.

22 RADIO SILENCE

Samantha wanted a ride. That was it. just a ride out of town. We both had plans to get the hell out of there. It seemed the least I could do to make up for shooting and almost killing her. I figured if I did her a favor, she would keep quiet about my little escapades. *That* was the least she could do since she tried to kill me and almost burned down my apartment building. She got on, under and everywhere in between my nerves like nobody's business.

The heater had kicked on full blast an hour earlier. Just to spite her, I hadn't dialed it down one bit. I guess I thought I could smoke her out, make her leave by sheer force of will. She was just as stubborn as I was. She sweated it out like a champ, didn't even crack her window. By the time we were a hundred miles out of town, her T-shirt was drenched. Still, she didn't budge.

We hadn't spoken or shouted at each other for over an hour. She crossed the line when she had called me a "lily-livered ass-wipe." I didn't even know what that was supposed to mean. But I knew, for her, it was the worst kind of insult. As of now, I was the worst kind of creep.

Why, you ask?

Here's what went down.

She blasts the radio. I turn it down. She turns it back up, mumbling insults under her breath. I turn it off. Strike one.

She's hungry. She's got to pee. I get her food and stop at a rest stop so she can do her business. She steals my wallet and buys a motherload of snacks and drinks and junk food after I've already fed her. Strike two.

Then, she pouts and cries and complains. And when I don't answer, she gets quiet. At a stoplight, she places something on the dashboard in front of me. Complacently, I look—and there it is, Julianna's name tag.

I swipe it up as if the whole world can see it, can sense how much it means to me. I cram it into my pocket, furious at her, but also strangely elated. And that makes me angrier. Strike three.

I scream at her, and she cries. I tell her how stupid that was and how we're tied to everything now.

She says nothing, except, "I just thought you might really want it."

I say nothing.

***

So, there we were, silent as two dead bodies laid out in one miserably small coffin. Not speaking. Both of us roasting to death in my overheated truck, willing to stick it out stubbornly until the end. I couldn't breathe, it was so hot. She must have been just as miserable.

The sun had come up long ago and was nestled high in the sky. I had to squint to see the road.

"Here," I heard her say. Next thing I knew, a pair of ladies' sunglasses were poking me in the arm. I glanced over and caught her staring, her wide eyes both sad and pathetic. Like puppy dog eyes that pulled you in and left you with a huge bill and a dumb dog you didn't want in the first place. I had made the mistake of looking and now I was stuck with a damn pet.

I shooed away the sunglasses, but she pushed back, insistent that I take them. "I don't want to die in a wreck, just because you wouldn't put these on," she said emphatically.

I took them and put them on, just to shut her up. She smiled up at me with a childish grin. I nearly wiped it off her face, but I didn't. Instead, I huffed as I peered into the rear-view mirror to get a look at myself. I looked utterly, utterly stupid. I felt even worse, staring at my unshaven face beneath those flowery pink sunglasses.

I grumbled under my breath, but it was nice to see the road without all that glare. So, I didn't grumble all that loudly. She noticed and smiled wider. Satisfied with herself, she wiggled comfortably in her sweaty seat and gazed out the window.

"Why do you kill people, Johnny?"

The question came out of the blue and struck me down like a lightning bolt. I'd never been asked that question before now. I'd never really thought about it. And now that the question had been asked so plainly, so nonchalantly, it seemed pretty mundane. An ordinary hobby like any other. It just happened to include lots of blood and sharp objects. The way she said it, passing it off as an everyday thing, made it seem—boring, conventional, and uncreative. I thought about my kill box again and felt ridiculous over how much of a struggle it had been for me to give it up. After all, the kill was what I was after—the bodies, my trophies. The trinkets left behind were nothing but a safety hazard.

"Johnny?" She said quietly, the sound of her voice broke my train of thought.

"I..." I started, unsure of where exactly I was going with this. "I...I don't know. I—"

Oh, come on, Johnny. This is an easy one. come on!

"I guess it's just a part of me that's always been inside, waiting to *do* something. To come to the surface and play. It just took me a little while to figure that out." The words seemed to tumble out of my mouth like water.

"How many have you killed, Johnny?" she asked, anything but hesitant.

I had to count for a minute.

Stupid boy. Doesn't even know his own body count.

"Nine. I have nine," The number teased its way from my lips like venom and thorns, choking me with every syllable.

I waited for her to be shocked or anything other than what she really was—utterly blank and empty.

She wasn't done asking questions, though. "*Had* nine. They're all gone now."

Short pause.

"Do you know who they were?"

Deep breath.

"Do you remember their names?"

Names? These girls had no names for me. I was in and out with them. Meet-cute and kill. Meet-cute and kill. There might have been an Ashley in there somewhere if I had to pick my brain, but I couldn't be sure.

"Don't you remember anything about them?"

Yeah, I remembered their bodies, their faces when I killed them. Their dead eyes when I was done with them. Dead was what I wanted them to be. Dead was how I liked best to imagine them. Dead bodies, dead eyes, dead girls.

Did I want to tell her that? No. But did I tell her that? Yes. I explained every detail of each girl that I remembered. Every last minute of each kill. Down to the millisecond when their eyes no longer shone with life and what I did with them after. I told her about #9 that wasn't really #9, because she wasn't my kill. Julianna—the one that I remembered the most.

Then, I waited anxiously for her to say something, to react. Her face was empty and emotionless. What the hell! I was sweating bullets while she seemed calm and cool.

Finally, she said, "You're different from everybody else, aren't you?"

I didn't like the way she said it, like there was something really wrong with me. Like I've said before, what's right for you may be really wrong for me. And what's wrong for you—morally and egregiously wrong—may be just right for me. It was just the way I was wired, probably from birth. I didn't think I had to apologize for being myself, the true and honest me. The animal, the predator, the beast. Everything in nature belongs to a pecking order. I just happened to be at the top of the food chain. At least I thought I was, until she asked that dumb question with that dumb tone of hers. Partially interested, mostly bored, and ultimately unimpressed.

It was a long and painfully awkward moment of nothing.

"That's alright by me," Samantha said softly.

We shared a glance. A silent moment together. The way she looked at me stirred up something in my gut that made me restless and unsure. Two things I just wasn't at all. Not ever, not until now. I turned away, clearing my throat of its nervous rattle, and I turned my attention back to the road. I stared it down like it was all I could see. Out of the corner of my eye, I saw her hand slowly and gently reach for me and settle on my leg. It wasn't sexual. It was just—nice. Like a warm hug. Not that I liked hugs or anything, but this was— nice. I let her hand stay there on my leg and we drove in silence for a long time.

23 A DEAD AND FAILING SWITCH

All this girl talked about was death. I mean every word out of her mouth was full of rage and hate and death. She really was fooling everyone with that defenseless good girl façade. And although I hated to admit it, she had fooled me too. Now that we were on the road, away from everything we both knew, she had turned over a new leaf. Evolved. Morphed into this little monster that was ready to pounce and strike at any minute. At least, she thought she was ready, ready to take on the world. But she was as green as the Iowa grass we had driven past. She didn't know real rage or that hunger that was all-consuming.

After all, she'd only killed one person—good old Dan—and that was an accident, so she said. She talked like an old war vet, but she had barely cut her baby teeth on him. Her hands were not yet dirty from the blood of it. It was just something for her to brag about, which she did every damn chance she got, as if somehow her measly little accidental kill amounted to anything next to my body count.

Fat chance.

I smiled to myself to think of it. She didn't notice; she was too busy gabbing. Her mouth ran like a motorboat, refusing to run out of gas. If anything gave a glimpse of what hell was like, this was it. Hours and hours of her taking up valuable space in my truck and sucking up all the good air to fill her big fat mouth.

My smile quickly faded.

You've got to lose her. Or—

No, I wasn't going to kill her. Not yet anyway.

*It would be absolutely deliciously wonderful. Just
think of it!*

And I did. A lot. There were hours of empty time in
my head as the miles stretched out before us. We'd
been cutting a clear path across the Midwest for a
while now. It was time for a change of scenery. A place
to settle down and settle in.

And I needed a break from all that chatter.

Yes, a long one.

She stopped for a split-second to take a breath and
I took the opportunity to fish the map out of the glove
compartment. My hand brushed her bare leg. Out of
the corner of my eye, I saw her smile. My only
response was to chuck the map into her lap and put
my hands back on the wheel, gripping it like a vice.
She maneuvered her skirt an inch higher up her thigh,
probably hoping I would see. I did, but she didn't need
to know that. I kept my eyes on the road and she
huffed quietly, wiggling her skirt back into its place.

I smiled then too. She noticed.

"You'd think I was your slave the way you treat
me," she muttered loudly as she fanned the map out
on her lap.

"Don't think of it as work," I said, still with a smile.
"This is a game. It's fun, I promise."

She looked at me, unconvinced. "What kind of
game?"

I leaned in close to her, just to tease her.

"Close your eyes," I said. I took up her hand in
mine, gently folding my fingers into hers. Softly, I lifted
her pointer finger. "And put your finger anywhere your
heart desires on the map."

"And?" She was still mad.

"And—that's your new home."

"*Our* new home," she corrected me.

She squirmed and squealed with childish delight
as she closed her eyes and pulled away from my touch.
She stuck her pointer finger up in the air, wiggled it

around the map and aimlessly circled with her fingertip.

"And the winner is..."

Bam!

Her finger plopped dramatically down to the left side of the map. She opened her eyes and we both took a glance down to where her finger was pointing.

"Devils Lake, North Dakota."

North Dakota? Wow. That really was the middle of nowhere.

Perfect.

I expected her to pout in disappointment, but instead, she was grinning from ear to ear. Her eyes were gleaming as she looked at me.

"Devils Lake, here we come!" A few seconds later. "How far away is that from here?"

"I don't even know where here is." I chuckled.

She opened her window and poked her head out. She waited like that until a sign appeared up ahead. She licked her lips and squinted as it came into view.

Wait for it. Wait for it.

"We're in River Valley!"

She contorted her thin body back into the truck and into her seat with a plop. She sighed with what seemed like contentment. Samantha was happy and, for once, she was quiet.

"Funny that it's called Devils Lake," she said thoughtfully. "Guess we're going to hell after all."

"Why would you go to hell?" I asked, playing dumb. With the hedonistic and hateful, evil thoughts this girl had rolling around in her brain, I was surprised that the devil himself hadn't risen up and snatched her by now.

She shrugged absentmindedly and said, "I killed somebody."

I tried not to laugh, until I saw the look on her face. She was proud of what she'd done, not afraid. But her "kill" didn't even count. It was just self-defense.

"That was self-defense. You didn't kill anybody. You just protected yourself."

She didn't seem convinced by my less than enthusiastic words.

"I wish I had really killed him then," she muttered, almost too low for me to hear.

"Why?"

She turned to me with black, angry eyes. I almost didn't recognize her. She shrugged again, and whatever darkness had clouded her face was suddenly gone.

"Guess you're going to hell for sure."

She pouted smugly, looking exceptionally pleased with herself for her cheap insult. I tightened my grip on the wheel, not liking the sound of that. I decided to keep quiet. She wanted me to come back with a retort, something snarky or even cruel. She wasn't going to get anything out of me. More pouting. And then—

"I have to pee."

"We're not stopping."

"But I have to *go!*"

"Shoulda figured that out fifty miles back."

What are you, her mother?

A huff from her turned into a long, exaggerated whine. She slapped her thighs and glared at me.

"Johnny!"

I laughed. I couldn't help it. Her face was so scrunched up and her nose wrinkled up in a childish look of consternation that looked cartoonish. She slapped me on the arm, trying to wipe the smile off her face. She couldn't though.

"Johnny, be good. Huh?"

Her words cut me a like a knife and frightened me. I felt my body shiver and shake. I gripped the wheel so tight I could hear its leather covering whine and creak beneath my fingertips. She could have said anything. Anything else would have been fine. But those three words set me off. I was a firework blasting off into the darkness, ready to explode on anything and anyone that got in my path. She tried to touch me again when I didn't say anything. I pushed her off. She shied away into a corner, biting her lip.

Johnny—

The voices of Julianna and my mother seemed to meld together into something dark and sinister in my mind. Their voices played on a loop living in the shadows of my brain like a threatening thunderstorm. Coming. Always coming. Closer and closer.

"Johnny."

Samantha was close. I didn't want her close. Didn't want to feel her body up against mine, the warmth and tension, an electric cord that struck every nerve, leaving me defenseless and lame. I pulled away from her and swerved to the side of the road. She nearly went flying out of the window.

Would've been better if she had.

Quiet. I just needed quiet.

We landed in a park and ride, next to a gas station and convenience store. Good, I could dump her here and just keep driving. She'd find her way. And anyways, what the hell did I care?

"Johnny?" she said again.

I didn't look at her. Didn't want to. I just kept my eyes ahead. Hell, I wasn't even blinking.

"Get on out of here."

She didn't.

"Go on, get out!" I reached across her lap and pushed open her door. "And don't you dare look back."

Her big, wide eyes batted tears down her cheeks. Without a word, she grabbed her purse and her shoes, and slid out of the car. She stood there just inside the door, holding everything she had in the world in her arms and looking at me with the saddest, emptiest gaze. She was lost. Lost without me. The god of her sick and twisted world of revenge and hate. The idol to which she held up her soul, ready to kill so that I would accept her.

You glean an awful lot from that little girl face she's putting on just for you.

Yeah, maybe. I saw it all there in those sad, sad, hungry eyes. God, this girl was getting to me. I screamed at her, and she backed away, slamming the door behind her.

I watched in the rear-view mirror as she walked barefoot toward the convenience store. I sighed, feeling the weight of her climb off my body. I could finally breathe. She was gone. I was me again, just me. Only I kept staring back in the mirror to watch her. She disappeared, probably into the store, and I could feel an aching itch settle in my stomach. I had to at least make sure she was alright.

Damn it, Johnny.

I threw open my car door with a world-weary sigh. "Damn it."

***

Ding!

The warm wave of heat rushed at me as I entered the convenience store. The lady at the counter smiled and nodded at me, but I wasn't interested in niceties. I was looking for that stupid girl down every aisle.

How big is this damn store?

And then—there she was in the corner of the store, her shoes and purse on the floor. She thumbed through magazines, her back against the magazine rack, flipping pages like nobody's business. She wasn't really reading them, not really looking at the pictures. She was buying time, looking busy, until they kicked her out.

I had to smile at that. She was smart, I'd give that to her. She knew how to survive. How to mesh with the crowd. How to fit in. She was pretty—alright, I admitted it. She had a unique spark of personality that couldn't be ignored. Maybe—just maybe.

Johnny, what are you thinking? Johnny!

I walked up to her without a word. She deigned to glance up at me from her magazine perusal, still angrily flipping the pages back. She was mad.

"You have to pee too?" she asked with an attitude and then she was back to her magazine with a flip of her frizzy hair.

I found her puerile rage amusing.

"No," I said. "And obviously, you didn't either."

She hung the magazine by its end and waved it at me as she rolled her eyes.

"Obviously, I came here for this."

I chuckled softly. She didn't like that and glared at me hard. It wiped the smile right off my face. I cleared my throat, but the words wouldn't come. I didn't know how to say what I wanted. She was just standing there, staring at me. So, I marched up to her, took her by the hand, and dragged her down the aisle.

She was able to grab up her purse before we were down the aisle and close to the front of the store. She was startled, but she went along willingly, almost gratefully. She didn't even worry about her shoes which we'd left behind. We passed the store clerk, who smiled a little more cautiously now. I nodded to her with a flashy smile and yanked Samantha outside.

Once we were out of the store, she pulled away from me. I realized then that the magazine was still clutched in her hand.

"Just what do you want, Johnny?" she demanded loudly.

Out of the corner of my eye, I could see the store clerk inside peering sideways at us. She looked concerned and reached for the phone. Quickly, I yanked Samantha by the arm and pushed her toward the truck. I forced her into it and slammed the door behind her.

One eye on the store, where the clerk was now on the phone and looking out the window, I hurried to the driver's side and hopped in. In a flash we were out of there, skidding out onto the highway.

"What the hell, Johnny?" was all she managed to say.

I didn't answer. I was too busy eyeing the road behind me for cops. Any minute now, they'd be flying up that road after me. Any minute now.

"Hey!" She snapped her fingers in my face and I grabbed her arm tightly.

"Don't ever do that to me! *Ever!*" I screamed.

"What am I now, your hostage or something?" she yelled.

"You tell me!" I yelled back in her face. "You're the one who doesn't seem to die. Disappear. Take a freaking hint. I want you gone in the worst way. So, you tell me, Samantha!"

She got quiet then. I couldn't read her silence and I didn't want to either. She was quiet and that's all that I cared about right now. But quiet was too much for her.

"That's the first time you've said my name. Really said it. Like ever."

I gritted my teeth. Figures, a girl would make this into some kind of freaking sentimental moment, when all I wanted was for her to freaking die.

"Johnny, why did you come back for me?"

I wanted to kill you myself, instead of leaving you for some other son of a bitch.

"It's cold," was all I could manage to mutter.

It was true. It was cold.

24 No Sleep and Night Talks

It was 3 A.M. and we'd been on the road non-stop for a while. I couldn't remember the last time I had slept. I just kept driving. The road up ahead, dimly illuminated by my headlights, had long ago blurred into the night. It seemed like the distant horizon had swallowed up the road and all that was left was sky and stars.

"What's the worst thing you've ever done?"

Samantha's voice caught me off guard. I had known she wasn't asleep by the constant fidgeting and rustling in the seat next to me, but it still startled me. I had to peel my eyes from the star-studded road to look at her. She turned to me with a dangerous smile.

"Like ever," she added.

"Isn't that obvious?" I said, a little too cocky. A little too proud.

She seemed unhappy and agitated by my answer, fidgeting even more in her seat. She took her feet off the dash and sat up straight, turning her whole body toward me.

Uh oh. This is serious.

She looked serious, alright. Like she was about to confess something herself. Instead, she said, "That doesn't count."

"It doesn't?"

"Pick something else."

I stuttered all over myself, clumsily spilling out, "Uh," as if it were the only sound I could make. She groaned with boredom and slumped back into her seat.

"Come on," she complained loudly. "You've got to have something."

Still stuttering, I finally just shook my head in answer. She didn't look pleased. She thought for a moment. I watched her wheels turning ravenously inside her head, until her eyes finally lit up with excitement.

"A secret! Tell me a secret! You're biggest one. The biggest, juiciest, most horrible secret you've got!"

That one is easy. My mother.

Don't go there. Johnny, don't!

I felt my mouth open slowly, the words creeping and crawling up into my throat. I held them back as long as I could, but the pressure of them pushed on my raw, exposed nerves, until I couldn't stand it anymore.

"My mother," I said abruptly.

She pushed me further. "What about your mother?"

***

"The flickering light of the green bathroom. The sound of the water running in the tub. My mother stands with her back to me, staring herself down in the mirror. From the crack in the door, I watch her step carefully into the tub. She doesn't see me. Doesn't notice. I am young enough to be afraid, but old enough to know good from bad. My mama is all bad. She closes her eyes with a sigh and leans her head back. Her arms are outstretched along the sides of the bathtub, her wrists tantalizingly bare and inviting.

"I wait. I'm good at waiting.

"I watch her fall asleep in the water, and then I creep in. Tiptoe slowly, as quiet as a ghost. Yeah, a ghost. I open the medicine cabinet above the sink. The cosmetic bottles inside begin to rattle. I hold completely still as she stirs in the water, groaning a little. But she's too drugged up on Valium to really wake up. I go back to my search and finally find what I'm looking for—a razor blade.

"I hold it carefully between my fingertips as I stand over my mother in the tub. The water ripples all around her as she stirs in her sleep. Gentle waves across her skin. The fluorescent light casts a strange sort of halo around her body, and she almost seems— good. Like a mother should. Until I look at her hardened, calloused fingers, the ones that hit and smack and touch me so painfully. I can feel the pain of them on my own skin as I look at them. I look at them until I can't look at them anymore. I focus my eyes on her wrists. If I look hard enough, I can see the dark blue veins. Teasing me. Calling me. Egging me on.

"I lick my lips, squeezing the razor blade between my two fingers. I edge my hand closer and closer to her skin. The blade is a breath away from it. I take a deep breath and let the blade rest on her skin, testing out the waters. She doesn't budge. Doesn't even flinch. Doesn't know what's coming.

"I gulp down the nervous acid in my throat. Sweat beads and drips down my forehead. A single drop falls to her arm like a teardrop, but there will be no crying today.

"Just do it, Johnny. It won't stop unless you do.

"The voice in my head startles me. It's never been there before. Whispers maybe, but never this loud. I don't want to listen, but I know what it's saying is true, and it fuels the rage in me. With one swipe, I make a clear cut across her wrist and another on the other wrist.

"Blood flows. Drips. It pools beneath her into the water and the water is a bright and vivid red. It's pretty and I stare at it for a long time, getting lost in it.

"I wait to see if she'll wake up. She never does. After a long while, I watch her sigh; it's raspy and rattles in her chest like thunder. And then, I know she's gone.

"I sigh, relieved. My chest doesn't feel so heavy, so tight with fear. I gently lay the razor blade next to her, but it slides into the water with a sickening plop.

"It's over. It's done. I go away. Far, far away into my room. Waiting for the morning. Waiting...waiting...waiting."

***

The words vomited up from my mouth like a tidal wave. A bucketful of filth from my ever-ready lips. At the end, I was breathless. I didn't even know if I'd made sense. It had been the birth of Mr. Hyde and the birth of whatever I had become. A monster. A villain. A devil in disguise. Whatever you called it, it had started on that day.

I glanced over at Samantha. Her eyes were wide but empty of the fear and the horror I had expected from my little tale.

"So, you killed your mother because she touched you?"

Deep breath. It sounded worse when she said it like that. With that teenage tone, utterly unimpressed, underwhelmed, and bored. I didn't answer her. I didn't think that kind of attitude deserved an answer.

We sat in silence for so long afterward that I got comfortable again. My mind relaxed from the torture of remembering my nightmare. I was content to watch the passing road signs and the landscape that passed by my window. The moon was new, barely a sliver in the sky, giving way for the stars to shine all the brighter in a blanket of twinkling luminescence.

It was—*beautiful*.

A far cry from my jagged memories that had cut through membrane and flesh like a saw. But I didn't have to think about it anymore now. Not ever again.

Deep breath in. Deep breath out.

"Do you wanna know my biggest secret?" Samantha's voice crashed into my consciousness like the rattling of a monster's cage.

"Sure," I replied against my better judgment.

"I'm pregnant."

Those two words shattered the quiet of the night. She wasn't done though with her surprises. She gave it a long, dramatic pause.

"That guy. The one I killed—"

"Dan."

"Yeah, Dan. It's his. He wanted me to get rid of it. I thought about it, but I kinda like the idea of having something to keep and cuddle and love. It's like having a real-live baby doll. Something that's all mine. That needs only me. Something I can pour all my love and hopes and dreams into. You know? I told him that night in the car that I was gonna keep it and he got real mad. I got tired of hearing him bitch about it, so I shot him."

She said that so matter-of-factly, so calmly and resolutely, that to me it felt like the right thing to have done.

Dan had been a bad, bad boy. He deserved what he got.

"He deserved it," I said.

She smiled at me, a soft and weary smile. The weight of the world was still on her shoulders. No matter how many miles stretched behind us, she couldn't erase that.

"Thanks," she said sleepily. "I thought so too. It's lucky I knew where he kept his gun."

With a smug little smile on her face, she curled up beside me to sleep, laying her head on my shoulder. It felt uncomfortable and wrong to have her so close, but the warmth of her small body against mine quieted my quick-beating heart. The smell of her soothed my aching head. So, I let her rest on me, while I put as many miles as I could between her past and mine.

25 THE ITCH AND THE CHASE

Forty-eight hours and no sleep. We stopped a lot and now I knew why. If she didn't have to pee, she was hungry. If she wasn't hungry, she needed to throw up. Needless to say, we weren't making much progress. We still had to about two hundred miles to go to get to Devils Lake. I wasn't going to last long at the rate we were going. I needed real food and a real bed to sleep in.

Samantha started to look feverish and pale. She was cold all the time, no matter how high I turned up the heat. We stopped more often for her to be sick. She puked so much I didn't know how she had anything left inside of her. Finally, I told her we were going to stop for the night.

"Where?" She said, her voice faint and weak. "There's nothing for miles."

I scoured the dark for anything up ahead. As if God or the universe heard me, there it was. A rundown old motel. Its sign was only half lit but the—

SL__PY T_ME M_TEL

—was going to have to be our home away from home for the night. I shot into the parking lot like a bat out of hell.

"Stay here. I'll be right back."

And then, I was gone. I hightailed it to the front desk, keeping my eyes on my truck. I leaned on the bell. From the window. I could see Samantha leaning her forehead on the window, her pale features pressed up against the glass.

Finally, a rough-looking old hag appeared behind

the counter.

"You want a room or something?" She spoke with a raspy croaking voice as she puffed hard on a cigarette.

There was an ashtray full to the brim with ashes and butts sitting next to her. She'd been at this all day. The little room was so saturated with the stench of smoke that I almost couldn't breathe.

I choked out a yes, got my key for the room, and hurried out, gasping for clean, cool air. I got Samantha into our room. Luckily, the only room available sported two twin beds crammed into the tiny, tiny space. I was thankful for that, and despite her previous advances, I think Samantha was too.

She collapsed onto the nearest bed and fell asleep almost instantly. I sat on the edge of mine, watching her. I needed to sleep, but I couldn't help feeling like if I did, the end of the world would come. Or at least, the end of all this. I couldn't shake that feeling.

Why do you care? She's just a stupid girl. One face among a million. Nothing special. Nothing you wouldn't kill.

"Stop it," I whispered loudly. Too loudly. Samantha stirred restlessly in her sleep at the sound. I clamped my mouth shut and tried to lie down, stuffing the pillow on either side of my head. I wanted to block out the noise in it, but nothing ever would.

My eyelids were suddenly as heavy as lead. I took one last look at Samantha lying still like a corpse on the small bed across from me, and then my eyes closed. I don't remember anything after that for quite some time.

I woke up hours later to the light of the bedside lamp glaring in my eyes. Samantha was sitting up, surrounded by chips, candy bars and mini donuts. A couple cans of Coke, both open and empty, were next to her on the nightstand. She was eating everything at once, sampling this bag, then that one, while she pounded on the television remote in search of something to watch.

TV snow. Then a fuzzy channel. TV snow. Then a news report that came in crystal clear. She stopped on it, turning up the volume.

"Virginia factory worker, Dan Wright, was found dead one week ago in his car near Blacksburg. Based on evidence found in his car, it is now believed that Mr. Wright was involved in several unsolved murders in the area. Police are looking further into the case..."

Samantha drained every drop of her Coke can and tossed it onto the floor. She laughed low and loud as she raised a mini donut to the television in a toast.

"Goodbye, Dan."

I couldn't help but chuckle under my breath. She realized I was awake and turned to me with a bright smile. She still looked flush, but her eyes had that mischievous sparkle back in them.

"We got him good, didn't we?"

I smiled in answer, still too tired to say anything. She kept eating her junk food snacks and surfing through channels. The room's solitary window was open, and the curtains pulled aside, letting in the freezing night air. Obviously, Samantha was hot again.

I pulled the covers over me, shivering and shaking. I tucked them under my chin as I stared out that window into the night and the darkness. As I watched, a lonely light flipped on, filling the parking lot with an eerie yellow glow. It was snowing outside, not enough to stick on the roads, but a slushy wetness was collecting along the sides. It was the kind of night that made you want to stay inside, warm, and safe in the quiet and the still. It reminded me of Christmas night, when the world nestles in its heavy sleep, and everything is still and peaceful. Except this was February, and nothing about this night was still or peaceful.

My body was already restless, shaking off its

blanket of sleep. I was ready for action and hungry. I glanced over at Samantha's treasure trove of snacks. Nothing in her lap looked appealing and I knew she wouldn't share. She was eating for two and I was an unwelcome third wheel at her feast. I would have to fend for myself.

I peeled myself out of the covers and the yellowed sheets. My face was damp and crusty. I must have drooled on myself. I wiped it off with the inside of my t-shirt and hopped off the bed. That little bit of sleep had done me good. I felt refreshed and alive. My stomach grumbled and growled.

Time to fill the tank.

I stumbled my way to the door with half-open eyes. I was almost outside when I heard her call to me.

"Where you going?"

Cringeworthy. Here I was, her actual savior and her only chance at a ride out of here, and she wanted to play house and keep tabs on me. So, I said, "What does it matter?"

She gave me this look like I was anything but right. Like I owed her, and she owned me. And I wasn't having that. I was anything but owned.

She must have seen the grimace on my face because her mouth now thickly coated in powdered sugar downturned into a shameless frown. That wasn't going to work on me. Not this time. So, I said nothing, just gave her the last remnants of a glare and stormed out, slamming the door behind me.

My god, that cold air felt good on my skin as I stepped out into the night. The snow fell softly down, brushing the bare skin of my arms and my face. Soft kisses on the wind to ease my aching, restless body and then the wind carried them away with a gravelly, hissing sigh. It was as if you could hear each snowflake grinding against the broken pavement. I smiled, but I felt eyes on me. I turned back to see Samantha at the window of our room, glaring me down. After a second, she shut the curtains with a resounding swoosh. The light and the warmth of our little place was gone, and I was alone in the dark.

Just how we like it.

A slow burning ache filled my body; it was hunger. A familiar hunger fueled by nightmares and rage. It was time.

That's right, Johnny. It's time.

Time to get my hands dirty.

Time for fun. Time to play.

Reset myself and remember what I was really here for.

Now to find our playmate for the night.

Easier said than done, Hyde. Easier said than—

Wait--

A yell swept across the parking lot, carried to me on the winter wind. Like magic, there she was. A tall, majestic redhead, a little rough around the edges in her tight leather pants and her peek-a-boo pink belly shirt. She had been crying, her black eye makeup smeared across half her face. Her cherry red lipstick was faded on her lips, a faint whisper of passion long past. Obviously, whatever she was walking away from was both the passion and the pain that reflected on her pale face.

She's perfect for you.

Yeah, perfect. And there it was, the itch. It rose in my body like a long-lost friend. It had been too long since it had stretched its legs and had a little fun.

The woman saw me looking and stared wide-eyed in my direction.

Like a deer in the headlights, ready to be captivated, caught, and killed. Captivate her, Johnny. Catch her and kill her.

I melded and molded my features to reflect her surprise, as if she caught me off guard too. Then I let a smile dabble lightly across my lips. A warm and welcoming smile that said "Hi, I'm just your friendly neighborhood country boy, ready to lend a hand and protect you."

She must have sensed it and felt safe as she crossed in front of me, because she smiled back. It was faint and barely there, her tears washing it away just as quickly as it came, but it was there. For me.

Captivated and caught. Now, boy, go get her.

She was heading toward the little sheltered area next to the motel office, where the vending and ice machines were located. It was a dimly lit area, hidden away between the office and the main building. A perfect place not to be seen. A perfect place to get lost.

I followed her into the little alleyway. By the time I rounded the corner, she was already at the vending machine, jamming her helplessly wrinkled dollar bill into the slot. It kept getting spit back out, no matter how she tried to smooth it out. She sighed and a fresh set of tears streamed down her face. She stamped her booted foot on the ground and whined under her breath, cramming the battered bill back into her back pocket.

Look at me. Come on, look my way, darling.

She looked at me, as if she heard me. A long, hard look like she was sizing me up and deciding if I was enough to save her. Enough for a good time for the night. Enough to help her forget her troubles. Evidently, I was, because she forgot about the vending machine and strolled up to me, her body shifting softly in the light and the dark.

She was about two inches taller than me, even in my sneakers. Was I intimidated? Absolutely not. Was she intrigued? Of course. What was there not to like? I was there in the night, looking her over like no one had in probably quite some time. Could she get anybody she wanted? Probably. But where were they? I was here. Me.

I'm here. Try me.

She sniffed, shivering in the cold, and wrapped her

arms around herself. Her red hair was long, cascading down her shoulders and back endlessly in loose curls. They caught on her neck, like a natural noose, ready to choke her, to confine her. She flipped them out of the way, but the wind caught them and put them back around her neck.

She eyed me with a lost look, dazed and empty. "You got a dollar?"

I smiled softly back. "I got more than that. Got a room and a warm bed. Just ordered some food. I just came out to get some ice."

She looked back at the motel rooms lined up like roach traps, ready to capture, catch and kill. She made a face like she didn't like that idea. So, I changed tactics.

"How about I drive you anywhere you like?"

Now I had her attention. She nodded. I smiled as I led her out of the alleyway, away from the light of the motel and out into the darkness. She willingly followed me toward my truck.

I could feel the surging hunger taking me over. Feel the monster taking over the man as my body silently prepared for a feast of the senses that it had been craving for oh so long. The taste of its sweet anticipation was intoxicating. I wanted more. I wanted the real thing. I started walking faster.

I heard her boots clip-clap faster on the pavement to catch up to me. I heard her chattering teeth as the wind picked up and a swirling gust of snow swept past us. Near my truck, I turned around to find her right behind me.

I smiled and said, "Where do you wanna go?"

"Anywhere but here."

I opened the truck door for her, and she was about to hop inside, when from across the parking lot, I heard that snotty, nasal voice yell, "Johnny?"

Damn it.

No, no, no. What the hell was she doing here now?

I glanced in the side mirror and saw her, swollen pregnant belly and all, waddling fast toward my truck. The redhead glanced at Samantha as she approached the truck and then at me with a look of confusion that quickly turned to disgust.

I moved to speak, opened my mouth and everything, but Samantha beat me to it.

"Honey, I thought you were getting the ice. What's going on?"

I glared her down. I could see the hint of a smile play across her lips. She was enjoying this farce far too much. She rubbed her belly vigorously, reminding all of us that she was carrying more than a heavy dose of guilt and shame.

"Nothing—nothing," the redhead quickly said as she scrambled out of my truck. She didn't even look my way. Instead, she turned to Samantha with as sincere an apologetic expression as she could. "I'm sorry, honey. I didn't know."

Samantha played her part well. She drudged up a few tears from the old trick bag of emotions. "Honey, what is this? And who is she?"

It worked. The redhead backed away from the truck, from Samantha, from me. "Look, I don't know what this is, but I'm not going to a part of it. I'm sorry."

And she was gone, hurrying across the parking lot. I watched her disappear into the night. And then, there was Samantha's laughter, devious and deliciously satisfied. It ground on my last nerve like sandpaper on glass. I whipped around to her with the worst look of rage I could muster. It wasn't enough to frighten her. She was having herself a good time.

I'd had enough. I grabbed her arm and yanked her back to our room, slamming the door behind us. She was still laughing when she reached under her shirt and pulled out a small bunched up pillow. She smoothed out her shirt and her swollen belly was gone.

Tossing the pillow to the bed, she said, "You're welcome."

I wasn't amused. I pulled her in by her shoulders, held her threateningly close so that she could feel the tautness of my muscles against her frail frame. That wiped the smile off her face.

"Johnny...I...I'm sorry, okay?"

I leaned close to her ear, trembling with rage. Through gritted teeth, I hissed, "Mess with me again and it'll be your body laid out like a feast for the maggots and the rats."

I pushed her away and she tumbled to the bed. Now it was her turn to tremble and shake, this time with fear. Her flushed cheeks paled, and her wide eyes watched me cross the room to my bed. I tumbled into it, wrapping myself in the cheap thin blankets with my back to her.

It was silent for the rest of the night. Somewhere in the early light of dawn, I managed to fall asleep, dreaming of blood and bone and the color red.

26 I REALLY HATE RAIN (OR THE STORM)

Two days later, we were parked at a motel in the middle of nowhere. It was late at night and the truck's windows were open all the way. It was raining. A hard, fast, drenching rain poured in like a deluge. We were just sitting there in the middle of this terrible winter storm, wet and staring at each other. Her blonde hair was plastered to her skin, and she was breathless.

We had fought across an entire state, mostly because she was pushing me to remember things. To remember the girls and their names and all the nitty gritty little details that she thought I had left out the first time. I resisted telling her more, no matter how much she begged, pleaded, and screamed. The more I kept quiet, the louder and angrier she got.

That landed us in this motel parking lot. I had run to the car from the motel office where had gone to get the key. Now here we were, sitting and staring.

I couldn't tell what she was thinking, and I didn't know if I wanted to know. Her lips wobbled open; she was trembling from the rain and the bitter cold. Trembling so hard that her teeth were chattering.

"What is it?" I finally asked.

She breathed in and slowly let it out. "It's my birthday."

I paused while I ingested her answer. "It is?"

She leaned into me until her lips brushed mine. I could feel her hot breath flowing into my open mouth.

It felt like the touch of a warm summer's day sunshine on your skin. It tingled through my body like a lightning strike.

"You know what my wish is?" she whispered, and every word tickled my ready lips.

I closed my eyes and waited for her to kiss me. I think I almost wanted it. But she didn't. She just hovered there like a ghost, vaporous and faint, almost not there at all. I felt the pull of her, the force of her body so close to mine. So strong, I thought she could suck my soul straight out of me, every sinewy strand of whatever made me who I was. And somehow, I surrendered, leaning into that pull until I trembled close to her.

"Tell me," I whispered back.

Her lips played around mine. So delicate. A seductive softness that rendered me weak. Then, like a hiss in my ear, she said, "To be anywhere but here with you."

The spell was broken, and I was shattered into a million pieces as I pulled forcefully back from her. She wasn't smiling, but there was a darkness in her eyes that seemed to smirk and sneer at me. Her lips were in a glossy red pout that I couldn't want. Not now. I felt ashamed for the feelings she had dredged up from my abysmal deep. Feelings and sensations that had not seen the light of day for ages. I hadn't felt anything for so long that I had forgotten I was human. For a moment she had made me feel like that was something I wanted. Now, I remembered why I had dug the hole and buried all that good and gone.

"You rotten little bitch," I growled at her.

She put on her mask of innocence once again, but it didn't work on me. Not anymore. That wide-eyed and trembling look of fear did nothing for me. I slapped her hard on the face and watched her reel back, stunned and shaking for real this time.

I wanted to see her tremble and shake. I wanted to

see her beg for my mercy and grovel at my feet. I
wanted to see her weak and defenseless at my hand of
power. I wanted to see all of her, flesh and blood and
bone, at my fingertips. Splayed open and rushing out
to blanket me. I wanted to own her, control her, and
kill her. I wanted—damn it, I wanted—

"What?" she exclaimed, though it came out like a
loud whisper more than a shout. She was staring me
down now, daring me to say what I really felt. As if she
knew already.

"Just say it!"

I didn't.

"What, Johnny? What?"

And she was close again, nearly on top of me. Her
face was in mine, but this time it was more
threateningly seductive or just plain threatening. I
couldn't tell anymore. The two were not polar
opposites in her, but the same side of the coin, the
same deep, dark color that was impossible to see
through.

"Don't you want me?" she hissed.

It took all of me not to pull her in and kiss her.
That's what I wanted. But what she didn't know was
that I had another side too. One she hadn't seen yet.
One that ruled the night and ruled me more than I
wanted to admit. That side of me, the side I'd kept so
very quiet up until now, was ready to play.

So, I leaned into her, threatening close, until she
almost backed down.

"Yes, I want you. So badly," I said softly.

She leaned into my touch. My lips. A sigh fell from
her lips. She was getting something out of this.
Something deep. This is what she wanted. Violent love.
Degradation and adoration all in the same bitter
breath. She was disgustingly sick, but I'd seen this
kind of lover before. I knew how to handle her.

I leaned in close. Closer. Closer still, until our lips
were touching. But I didn't kiss her, just grazed the

flesh of her lips, and smiled.

"Splayed out and dead. Your blood on my fingertips. With everything, all of you, as mine."

I expected her to back away from me, even just a little. She didn't. Instead, she kissed me hard and passionately. So hard I could feel her bite my bottom lip and the taste of blood trickled to the back of my throat.

"You'd like that, wouldn't you?" she said sharply.

She glared me down like a guard dog ready to attack. Like she wasn't afraid of me or what I could do.

I smirked and said, "Honey, you have no idea what I could do to you. And no one would even find you."

She swallowed hard, blinking blankly in the silence. She leaned in close to my ear and hissed out, "I know exactly who you are. *Exactly* who you are."

A threat?

How nice.

A devilish grin spread across her face, while big baby doll tears rolled down her cheeks. The effect was both confusing and terrifying; the fact that she could perfectly encompass both emotions at once was unnerving.

"How?" I asked, almost mocking her.

With a playful look, she said, "I feel like I know you, Johnny, like I know myself. We're two parts of the same beating heart. The same mind."

Danger, Johnny! Danger!

Yeah, danger, alright. I had myself a sick psycho on my hands. A weirdo of the worst kind. She wasn't just my own personal stalker. She was a fan.

27 #1 Fan

I waited for an answer to the question I had yelled in her face. When she didn't answer after about two minutes, I screamed it again.

"What makes you think you know me?"

Her eyes lowered with a sly sort of batting of her lashes. The rest of her face was hidden in the shadows; I couldn't see her features, her mouth, and that unnerved me. There could be anything in that dark. A smile or a sneer like the devil catching a very stupid man in a deathtrap.

"Answer me, Samantha!"

Her smile faded and it seemed that the glint of curiosity in her eye grew into a blazing bonfire. She was drenched from head to toe and the rain just kept coming. Her hair was matted to her flushed cheeks, and she trembled wildly in the cold. It was the first time I had seen her cold, and for some reason it hit me in the pit of my stomach. I couldn't let her be cold, so I grabbed a hoodie I had crammed in between us, blissfully dry and warm from being sat on. I didn't say a word as I handed it to her. There was nothing to say.

Wrapping herself in the hoodie, she brought the frayed and faded sleeves to her face, smelling them and savoring the rough feel of the fabric. She breathed in that disgusting hoodie like it was top notch perfume. I couldn't believe what I was seeing.

"Can I keep it?" she asked hungrily.

I couldn't believe what I was hearing either. This girl was creeping on me in ways that even I wasn't prepared for, and I knew all about creeping. I had to take this slowly, so I didn't piss her off. There was no telling what she was capable of or what she might be thinking of doing.

"Samantha..."

Good, Johnny. Say her name. Keep saying it and maybe she won't bite.

Not helpful, but I would give it a shot.

"Samantha, how do you know me? And how much do you know?"

She sniffed and nuzzled the hoodie a little more, before she cooed softly, like a lover confessing her affection. But this was far from that. At least, I think it was. She wagged her finger at me with a look that said she was enjoying every damn minute of this.

"No, no, no, Johnny."

I didn't listen. I grabbed for her arm, but she swiped the side of my face, scratching me deep with her jagged fingernails. She frowned at me playfully.

"Johnny, be good."

I gritted my teeth hard as I said, "How the hell do you know that I won't slice you open, right here and now?"

She grew pale for a second. "I know who you are and where you're from, Johnny. And I know about all of them. All the girls. From your lips to my ready ears, honey. You threaten me and I'm one step away from turning you in. I'll do it too. There's a payphone right over there. I can do it."

Careful, Johnny.

Careful? Careful of what?

Be careful that she doesn't get under your skin. Ask yourself what her angle might be. When you look at her, remember. Remember all those pretty, pretty girls. Their blood spilling out like every good thing you can imagine. Like Christmas and birthdays—yes, they were your presents. Don't let her take that from you. Johnny? Johnny?

"Johnny?"

Her snotty, nasal voice broke through my thoughts, and I came out of them like through a tunnel, vast and abysmal. The storm clouds had shifted, and the rain was riding a fast-track lane right into my side of the car. I was drenched, the cold and hard rain pelting me as if to punish me. In that moment, I felt the heavy weight of the universe, watching me and judging me for everything I had done. Did I feel guilty? Did I feel anything at all for all the pain I had probably caused?

No.

"No," I said curtly.

That's all I said. I got out of the car and slammed the door behind me, marching out into the rain toward the room I had rented for the night. The rain was coming down harder, thunder rumbling overhead that was deafening. Still, I heard her car door slam shut and her plodding footsteps slosh through the puddles toward me.

"What do you mean?" she yelled. "Johnny?" She screamed when I didn't answer her. "Why are you so angry?"

Angry? I was furious. Enraged to the point of madness. It wasn't that she was pretty, and that the more I looked at her, I wanted her. It wasn't any of that. It was—it was—

"Johnny?" she whispered.

Her voice was nearly lost within the roar of the storm. But I heard it. The sound made my skin tingle and crawl. I couldn't tell if it was with pleasure or fear. Nevertheless, I turned back to her. She was right behind me, just staring up at me in the rain with eyes as big as saucers. Tears ran wilder than the rain down her reddened cheeks. She was sniffling and she looked feverish.

"Johnny..." she said again faintly, her voice trailing off.

All I remember seeing in that moment were her

lips, rose-pink and trembling. They pulled me in, body, eyes, and all. I pulled her in, nice and tight, and kissed her. The kiss was like fire and ice, melting and colliding and simmering into a blistering mess. As our lips touched, the lightning crashed wildly overhead for a full half a minute. One strike after another in rapid succession, illuminating the blackness. I felt like it set my insides on fire and my heart was racing.

Bom-bom-bom-bom-bom-bom!

The sky went dark. I pulled away from her touch, her lips, every part of her. She clung to me, her fingernails digging into my side and pulling me in for more. I let her kiss me again, much harder, and more violently, as if she couldn't get enough. As if she was sucking the life right out of me. And I let her.

Finally, she pulled away slightly, her lips still next to my skin so that I could hear her every quickened breath.

"Johnny," she whispered again.

It made me tremble. I looked her in the eye, just in time to see her eyes roll back into her head. Her body collapsed into my arms. I lifted her up and carried her. Running, I was running. To the room I had rented for the night. With the girl I couldn't seem to kill.

"Samantha!"

28 Losing Touch (or the One I Couldn't Kill)

The rain had stopped. I lay in the dark next to Samantha, listening to her breathing. Her breaths were coming faster and faster. She was asleep or unconscious, I couldn't tell, but I kept one hand on her chest to make sure her breathing didn't stop. It was one in the morning, and I hadn't slept at all. I was fighting to keep my eyes open, though the dark was so deep that I couldn't see anything anyway. I was so tired that I could barely tell if I had drifted off for a minute.

Needless to say, I was worried. Worried that I would soon have a dead girl on my hands in this rented room. Another problem for good old Johnny to figure out. Whatever was going to happen, I would have to figure it out fast.

Well, it's simple, Johnny. You have two choices. Let her live or let her die.

"If I let her live?" I answered the dark.

That's easy. You'll have a pandora's box to take care of. Open her up and you'll have one hell of a plague on your hands.

Oooph! Good point.

"What if I let her die?"

Silence.

"What if?"

Second thoughts, Johnny? That must have been one hell of a kiss.

But it wasn't the kiss. It was—

"Her."

It *was* her. I peeled back the layers of my brain and realized it had been her all along. She was there, in my every memory.

My almost #4. I remembered her face among the girls around the fire as I tried my hand at flirting with the night's catch.

She was the *real* #4 there in the store as I met that hairy-legged freak at the counter. The one that welcomed me into the city.

She was #5 there at the factory where I worked. She was there when that girl asked me out.

She was #6 in the hallway as I left the girl's apartment. And again, just outside. I was afraid someone might have seen, might have heard. But no one followed me that night. So, I thought.

She was #7 walking just behind the girl in the fog. I remember seeing her staring straight at the girl, not at me. That stupid smile spread across her face.

She was #8, the girl and I passed her in the hallway of my apartment. Her eyes were on me like a hawk. It unnerved me at the time.

But I hadn't thought anymore about her. About seeing her. She was just another nameless, faceless girl in the crowd. One that I wasn't particularly attracted to at the time. One that I didn't want.

That's not the question you should be asking. Why the hell is she everywhere?

My hand on her chest no longer rose and fell in steady repetition. It didn't move. Dear god, she wasn't breathing. I jumped to my knees, hovering over her. I shook her hard, trying to wake her. To bring her back. Her face was pale, almost blue in the faint moonlight peeking through the half-closed curtains.

I bent down to hear her heartbeat, but there was none. I pounded on her chest, pressing harder and harder. Nothing revived her. Blood soaked the white sheets on the queen-sized bed we were sharing. Blood from her bullet wound. The wound I had given her when I shot her.

God, I had done a number on this one. I had really, really screwed up.

Now she was dead.

What's that? Tears? Are you crying? You big baby, she was just a girl. Another stupid girl in your way.

"No!" I screamed. "She was different. She was— *Her.*"

No, no, no. Julianna was the one. You're mixing things up! You don't understand--

"No!" I cried out against the darkness, and it grew quiet.

All I could hear was the sound of my own heart beating too fast, my breathing, heavy and erratic. I looked down on Samantha's body and I nearly screamed. I had never been afraid of death. Never in all my life. I had reveled in it, swam in its murky depths, and celebrated it. Now—now it made me sick to look at it. Sick and utterly revolted. I could feel the revulsion creeping up my throat. I choked it back down and took Samantha's dead body into my arms.

I stumbled my way to the tiny bathroom and kicked the door open wide. The tile floor was chipped and filthy. Grime and hair and questionable stains were everywhere I laid my eyes. The bathtub was just as disgusting, a red rust ring coating its rim. That didn't bother me. Nothing did, except the dead girl in my arms.

My mind was hazy and feverish. It took every ounce of concentration and strength to step into the bathroom. Every step leading toward the pale green bathtub with its flickering fluorescent lights above it like a spotlight. Like twinkling stars, watching, and waiting and whispering. They knew what I was going to do. They knew the girl was dead. They knew that it was me. They knew—they knew.

At the foot of the tub, the light above flickered like

it was on its last leg, its illumination fading to near darkness. I stared that tub down like it was a monster about to leap up to get me. It was empty, but I could still hear the water sloshing inside. Hear something heavy and solid bumping the sides like the rocking of a boat on hard ocean waves.

That was it. I couldn't take anymore. I gently laid Samantha in the tub. I looked down on her pale and lifeless face, her eyes open just slightly. Enough for me to see her dilated pupils, her deep blue irises staring up at me. I ran. Ran from the room and headed toward the door like the devil was on my heels. He was. He was coming. Coming to collect me for all my bad deeds. I wasn't good. I was never good. God, the devil, and the whole freaking universe knew it now.

Something stopped me from running out of the motel room. The rain had started again. I could hear it pounding against the door, splattering, and sliding to the pavement.

Johnny?

The sound of Samantha—the sound of Julianna—the sound of my mother—all rolled up into one terrible moan, rushed at me like a tidal wave. I shook my head violently to try and get it out. To erase the pull it had on me, the fear it created. I was trembling all over now, afraid to turn around and see whatever horror there was to see.

Johnny, be good. Be good, Johnny.

I was crying now. Fat, ugly tears streaming down my face. But I still didn't turn around. I didn't want to see *Her.* I didn't want to see Samantha—Julianna—Mama. I didn't want to see them. I didn't want to face what they had become in this dark, dark night.

I closed my eyes tight, wishing away the rain and the voices and the darkness. I could still hear that damn water running in the tub, that steady bom-bom-bom of the heavy bodies in it as they sloshed inside. Bodies, all of them drowned. All of them bloody and slit. All those girls. All of them. All the ones that I had killed. All the ones before that I had wanted to kill. All the ones that died on my watch. Dear god, *all of them!*

They were all there in that bathroom. In that overflowing tub. Waiting for me to join them. From that room, from the darkness inside, there came a low, rumbling hum that seemed to vibrate along the walls and the floor toward me. It consumed my body, and I shook in its wake. Slowly, the rumble turned into a sound, and the sound turned into words. A word. Over and over and over again.

Rotten.

It hissed in my ear, the sound shooting through me like an arrow. It pinned me to the floor where I stood, and I couldn't move or make a sound. They were coming. I could hear the squeal of flesh on the porcelain tub as they pulled their way out. The plodding of damp flesh on the tile. Coming nearer and nearer. I listened as their footsteps gathered at the bathroom door and with a hiss, I heard their shuffling feet on the carpet. Closer and closer.

Johnny!

Screamed on the air like a banshee call. I clamped my hands over my ears as I leaned against the door. Whimpering, I made myself turn to look at them. If I was going to go out, then I was at least going to see it to the end. And there they all were. All of them. Too many to count. They filled the room with their revolting smell of death and decay. They filled the darkness with their dead, dark eyes. They stared me down with all the hate and malice and ill-will they had.

I looked on each face. Remembering every moment with them. Every last drop of their blood I had spilled. Every moment I had carefully constructed their flesh into my playthings, my weapons against the shame I felt in myself. That was always there, haunting me.

I screamed.

Screamed bloody murder until I'd emptied every

ounce of breath from my lungs. There was no safe place away from them. No place except—I made a beeline for the bathroom, dodging their bloodied, broken bodies that swung like a pendulum toward me. They were coming for me. Coming. I stood just inside the bathroom and laughed in their face as I slammed the door shut tight and locked it against them.

Backing away from the door, I could hear them clawing at the door. Screaming my name. That door wouldn't hold them back for long, I knew that. I searched in the darkness for something, anything that I could use as a weapon. The medicine cabinet above the sink. I rushed to it and yanked it open, old cosmetics and bottles from old guests tumbled out. There it was, amongst the pile in the sink: a straight edge razor. With trembling fingers, I grabbed it up.

I stumbled and fell, curling up into a ball next to the tub.

So, this was it. This was the end. The end of everything. The end of me. All my effort, all my work, for this moment. This moment right here, where I literally had lost my shit, and anything left of my sanity. I was in this room with a dead body. One I didn't kill. Outside of this room, all that was left for me were the dead and decaying bodies of all those women. Waiting for me. Waiting for me to die. I didn't want it to end this way. Being killed by my own terror or the demons that were chasing me. I didn't want it to end this way.

You've got everything you need right there in your hand, Johnny. Everything you need to end it on your terms.

Hyde was talking about the razor. I had forgotten I was holding it. Looking down, it glistened even in the dark, like a shiny new present. Ready to be enjoyed.

I gulped the air, staring down what seemed like my only option. I didn't like it. I didn't like the way its glossy finish stared back at me with a sneer across its signature curved blade. But the smile was on my own reflecting back at me. I was smiling. My god, I was smiling. No, I was laughing.

The warbled sound of my laughter split in two, then three, and became the laughter of my mother and Julianna, as if they were in on this little joke. They were in the room now. In the corner. In the shadows. Watching me and waiting. Well, I would give them a show.

Gripping the blade tightly in my trembling hand, I brought it to my skin. Let it hover there. Deep breath in and then—

"Johnny?"

Samantha's faint voice tumbled to my ears like a gunshot. I shot forward, scooting away from the tub as fast as I could on the grimy tile. I watched the tub, watched as a hand and then an arm fluttered up and out. It gripped the side of the tub and up came Samantha, looking pale and still a little blue.

Alive. She was alive.

She looked frightened and confused, her eyes going everywhere at once to get her bearings. Then they turned to me. Dark eyes accusing me, judging me.

Her. She knew everything. Knew all my secrets, all my bad things. I didn't have to die. She did.

"Johnny, what happened?" She pleaded, looking more and more frightened as the seconds passed.

She saw the blade in my hand and shook her head, scooting as far into the tub as she could, as if that would save her from me. Clinging to the razor blade, I lunged forward with a scream that could have woken the dead. Maybe it did. All the same, my body loomed over her. The blade came down.

It stopped just short of her throat. I wasn't having second thoughts. No, not me. It was her eyes. Her eyes frightened me. They were vivid and bright and wide, full of life and beautiful. Something about the life in them made me afraid.

The blade brushed her skin and she winced, breathless and weeping. Those vivid eyes were draped in tears. I had done that. Like I had done to countless others. Why was this one different?

Because I knew her name. I knew her. Damn it, I knew her. And that made all the difference.

I pulled my hand away, and a deep breath tumbled from her chest. I stumbled back into the shadows. There in the shadows with my mother and Julianna. There in the dark where I belonged. Tears were falling from my own eyes now. Streaming down like a torrent of rain. Samantha looked at me. And I looked at her. Nothing was said. It was as if we both knew this is how it needed to end. It had to end. It had to end. I had to.

My mouth opened to speak. The words spilled out. "Don't remember me."

And then, slit! slit! Wrists bleeding. Blood oozing. Pouring. Running. Pooling all around me on the yellowed tile. I laid back and let it come.

29 To the Future Me

The morning sun was just cresting the horizon as I reached the sign for Devils Lake, North Dakota. I let out a whooping holler as a smile spread across my face, jumping up and down in my seat in the truck. The radio was blasting, and the windows were rolled down, so that the clear cool air could brush across my face.

I raised my orange soda to the sign in a toast.

"Here's to a new start and a new me! Everything is better in Devils Lake. I know it!"

Johnny's razor blade was tucked neatly under my seat.

Just in case.

Of course, I had to giggle at that. There would definitely be a case. Many cases. Many uses for such a damn good blade.

I rolled into town doing twenty over the speed limit. Reckless? Maybe. Fun? Damn right. I was laughing my head off as I sped past helpless bystanders and pedestrians, who dodged out of the way of my fabulous driving skills. But I saw every one of them look my way. I was already turning heads. Making a scene. It was fantastic!

I drove straight through town, seeing the sights, which took all of five minutes. I blinked and I was at the city limits. Damn. Not what I expected. I glanced back at Devils Lake, North Dakota in my rear-view mirror and grimaced with utter boredom and disgust. This wasn't the town for me. It wasn't even the right state. I needed something warmer. Something with sights and sounds and people.

Goodbye, Devils Lake!

I pounded my foot on the gas pedal and sped out of there like a bat out of hell. Ready to see what the day might bring. Anything was possible. Just about anything.

The miles stretched out before me, the flat country yawning into mountains and valleys. I didn't care if I got lost. I probably was. I didn't know where the hell I was. I just kept driving. Driving far away from anything I had ever known. From all of that dark stuff that had kept me stuck in one place for far too long. I was driving now to the future me and whatever that might mean. Whatever that might be.

And then I saw *Him.* A beautiful specimen of a man, rock solid and mountainlike. Built like a god and handsome as hell. His car was along the side of the empty road, smoke billowing into the air like a signal. It was for me. I knew it.

So, I slowed my truck down alongside him and hung my head out of the open window.

"Looks like you're stuck," I said, with all the southern charm I could muster and a killer smile to match.

He smiled. It was a pretty smile.

"Looks like," he said, looking down the road to see if there were any other cars coming his way.

None. None at all. He turned to me with a sigh.

"You wanna ride?" I made sure to lean over the window, so that all my best assets were in plain sight.

Hey, girl's gotta do what she's gotta do, right?

His eyes weren't on my face. Bait taken.

"Where ya headed?" he asked, stepping closer to my truck.

"Anywhere but here," I said with a coy smile.

He thought about it for a moment. "Sounds good to me."

I let out a little giggle just for him as he went

around the front of the truck to the passenger side. He liked it, I could tell. He liked me too. I could tell that too.

This is too easy.

He hopped into the truck and turned to me with a smile as he held out his hand to me. "Name's David."

David, David, David. His name is David.

I wanted to remember his name. Remember his smile and the way his eyes were when they looked at me. I wanted to remember everything about this moment. So, when I killed him, I would have that to hold onto forever. When he looked away to pull the seatbelt down, I felt under the seat for the razor blade. Just to be sure.

Don't worry. I'll make it special for you, David. After all, you're only my second.

His seatbelt clicked and he was ready. So was I.

Patience, Samantha. All in good time. First, let's give him a ride to remember.

"Ready?" I said with a silly grin, gripping the wheel with excitement.

"Ready."

I put the car in gear. "Ready!"

ABOUT THE AUTHOR

Keshia C. Willi was born and raised in the mountains of the Shenandoah Valley in Virginia. Her writing has been a lifelong journey which has led her down many paths, including script consulting and screenwriting, for which she has been recognized in several national script competitions. Virginia is still her home, where she lives with her husband and four dogs.

Houseofhonorbooks.com

BOOKS BY THE AUTHOR

Fire Tales

Coming Summer 2023

Beware the Wolf
A short story collection

Made in the USA
Middletown, DE
16 July 2023

35289905R00116